For Gabriel,
Max and Dom.

First American Edition 2019
Kane Miller, A Division of EDC Publishing

Polly and Buster: The Search for the Silver Witch
Text & illustration copyright © 2019 Sally Rippin
Series design copyright © 2019 Hardie Grant Egmont
First published in Australia by Hardie Grant Egmont

For information contact:
Kane Miller, A Division of EDC Publishing
P.O. Box 470663
Tulsa, OK 74147-0663
www.kanemiller.com
www.edcpub.com
www.usbornebooksandmore.com

Library of Congress Control Number: 2019946512

Printed and bound in the U.S.A.
1 2 3 4 5 6 7 8 9 10
ISBN: 978-1-68464-095-9

The Search for the Silver Witch

written & illustrated by

SALLY RIPPIN

A DIVISION OF EDC PUBLISHING

What Came Before Now

*P*olly Proggett is a witch and her best friend, Buster Grewclaw, is a monster. But they live in Blackmoon Coven, where witches usually don't mix with monsters, and their friendship has led them into all kinds of trouble.

Polly and Buster have been on the run from Deidre Halloway, the leader of the Witches Against Monsters movement, who has somehow gotten it into her mind that Buster is *dangerous*. Polly's favorite teacher, Miss Spinnaker, hides Polly and Buster at her mother and stepfather's house, deep in the Amber Skull Forest, and heads back into Blackmoon Coven to try to set things right. But when she doesn't return, and Mrs. Halloway turns up on their doorstep, our two friends decide they have to take matters into their own hands.

Following the directions she receives from her *magic stones*, Polly heads into dark and dangerous territory, first escaping from a gang of angry monsters, then a mine full of spooky ghosts, always with her best friend, Buster, by her side.

Polly is overjoyed to find her father's ghost deep in the mines. He explains that a *mythical gorvan* was accidentally woken in the mines and its mist has been making witches and monsters hate each other. Polly does the spell he teaches her to put the gorvan back to sleep. Now that the gorvan's mist is no longer infecting the town with its badness, Blackmoon Coven should go back to the peaceful place it once was … Shouldn't it?

One

"Mom, I'm *fine* to go back to school today," Polly Proggett says, sitting down at the breakfast table. "Really!"

"Are you sure?" Polly's mother frets as she places a steaming pot of nettle tea and a plate of toasted jackarons in front of her. "You don't look well. And you hardly ate any of the lizard broth I prepared for you last night." She wrings her hands as she fusses around Polly, who is sitting neatly in her pressed school uniform. "Maybe you should stay home a bit longer? I'm happy to take another day off work to look after you."

Polly shakes her head. For the first time in her life, she is *dying* to get back to school. She's been grounded ever since Miss Spinnaker brought her home from the mines, and hasn't been allowed *any* visitors. Not even her best friend, Buster! With no TV and no one to talk to, these last few days have felt like the longest, boringest ones ever. Besides, she has to prove she's well enough to go to the Mayor's medal ceremony this weekend. It's not every day your best friend receives a medal for bravery!

"Mom, seriously, I'm fine!" Polly says for the millionth time. She picks up a jackaron and inspects it for any lumpy bits. Polly hates jackarons – even if they *are* good for you. Her mother never grinds the caterpillars up finely enough and their legs get caught in her teeth.

She closes her eyes and remembers Mortimer's monster flipcakes, smothered in Flora's magical sparkle syrup. Thinking about them makes her heart **squeeze with happiness.** It's hard to believe she and Buster ate them only last week – it feels like *such* a long time ago.

Polly is desperate to talk to Buster about everything that happened. He is the only one who was with her for the whole journey. Not even Miss Spinnaker, her favorite teacher, knows the truth. Polly knows she will have to tell her eventually, but she has to find the right way to do it. She can't risk being expelled from Miss Madden's Academy for doing spells out of school! Her mother would never forgive her.

Polly's big sister, Winifred, slinks into the kitchen and grabs the biggest jackaron as she sits down. "Mmm! These jackarons are *delicious*, Mom!" she says enthusiastically, shooting a glare at Polly as she takes a big bite and chews loudly in Polly's ear.

Winifred was nice for almost *three whole days* after Polly returned. But now that Polly is safely home, with no greater injuries than a few grazes on her cheeks and a fading bite mark on her hand, Winifred has returned to her usual eye-rolling and annoying self.

"Oh, thank you, darling," Mrs. Proggett says, smiling. "I used fresh maggots this time. They make a *much* smoother paste and they are *so* good for you!"

Polly watches her sister spit a mouthful of chewed-up jackaron into her napkin when their mother's back is turned. Caterpillars are one thing, but no young witch can pretend they like **maggots**. Not even Winifred! She reaches past Polly for the box of Crispy Toad Flakes.

Polly **giggles.** She is happy to be back with her family after such a long time away. She slips the rest of her jackaron to Gumpy, their pet bortal, when no one is looking. "I'd better go pack my bag," she says, pushing back from the table. "I don't want to miss the bus."

Her mother spins around from her spot at the sink. "Oh, I'll drive you this morning," she says quickly, wiping her hands on a dish towel.

"Cool!" Winifred says, but Polly frowns. Their mother *never* drives them to school. Not even when it's hailing!

"Mom. It's OK," she says kindly, though she's also feeling a bit frustrated by her mother's fussing and fretting. "I'm fine to get the bus. Besides, I want to see Buster."

Winifred stops her noisy chewing and the kitchen is suddenly very quiet. Polly sees a strange look pass between her mother and sister.

And right then and there, she knows that something is not right.

Two

Polly's mother has a weird expression on her face that makes Polly's tummy curl with worry. "Mom? What's going on?"

"Polly," her mother says, her voice coming out awkward and strained. "I'm sorry to have to say this, but you're not to play with Buster anymore. Nor any other monster, for that matter."

Polly snorts. "What are you talking about, Mom? Buster is my friend. My *best* friend. You know that." She looks to Winifred for support, but her big sister turns away, cheeks reddening.

Polly's mother sits down and takes Polly's hand in hers. Her eyes are **full of fear**. "I really didn't want to tell you this, darling, but over the last few days things between witches and monsters have gotten much worse. They are saying on the news there's going to be a war in Blackmoon Coven. I'm sorry, Polly, but it seems Mrs. Halloway was right. Some monsters *are* dangerous."

"What?" says Polly in disbelief. **"But that's not true!"**

"It *is* true, Polly!" Winifred says, her eyes lighting up with drama. "You can't trust *any* monsters anymore."

"That's ridiculous!"

Polly sputters. "Buster and his family are good monsters. You know that! Mrs. Grewclaw brought over soup when you were sick. There won't be a war. Mrs. Halloway has gone." Polly remembers how angry the Amber Skull Forest Gang were toward Deidre Halloway. "*She* was the one stirring up all the trouble. And the Mayor is giving Buster a medal for *bravery* this weekend. Why would she do that if monsters were *dangerous*?" She feels her voice rising in frustration.

Polly's mother sighs. "The medal ceremony has been canceled," she says sadly. "Mayor Redwolf thought it was too dangerous to have such a large gathering of witches and monsters while things are the way they are. I'm sorry, darling," she says, reaching out to stroke Polly's hair.

"But that's not fair!" Polly says. "Buster *earned* that medal rescuing Malorie from the mines! He's a hero! Everyone in Blackmoon Coven should know this by now. If Buster receives that medal it will prove monsters aren't dangerous!"

Polly's mother drops her hand into her lap, anger flashing across her face. She stands up and clears the table to show their conversation is over. The plates clatter together noisily, and Gumpy runs out of the kitchen in alarm.

She turns to look at Polly again, her cheeks flushed. "Polly, you disappeared for *two* days with that monster from next door and I had *no* idea where you were! For all I know he could have *kidnapped* you! I was *sick* with worry and I am *not* going to let that happen again. So you are to stay away from *all* monsters. *Especially* Buster. Do I make myself clear?"

Polly sits at the table with her mouth open, gasping like a fish.

Her mother repeats the question, lower and slower. "Polly. Do I make myself clear?"

Polly drops her eyes. "Yes, Mama," she mumbles. Her thoughts are **fizzing loudly**, but there is no point in arguing. Polly knows her mother is only angry because she is afraid. And it is Polly who made her this way, by running away with her best friend.

Polly wishes she could tell her mother everything that happened – how she was called to the mines by the ghost of her father, and how she did a spell to put the gorvan back to sleep to keep the town safe. She wishes she could tell her how brave Buster was and how he stood by her side no matter what. Even when he was more scared than she was.

No, there is no point in upsetting Mama any more than I already have, Polly tells herself. *This will all settle down soon. It has to!* And she reaches down to tap the little lump in her school tunic for luck.

Tucked away there, deep in her pocket, is the little silk pouch her mother gave her after her father died, with the *three magic stones* inside. Her father's ghost promised Polly if she kept them safe, the gorvan could never trouble them again.

Polly knows she must protect these stones with her life.

Three

As they drive along their street, Polly sees Buster sitting in the bus shelter in his overalls. The sky is heavy and gray clouds roll across the sun. Polly's mother starts up the wipers as a light rain streams across the windshield and the windows fog up from the warmth of the car.

A witch on a motorized broomstick zips past them, head bowed to avoid the rain.

Polly notices that the bus shelter is covered in fresh graffiti. Big spray-painted tags of the letters: *M* or *W*. *M* for monsters and *W* for witches. Polly's heart shrinks. When did their world become so angry and mean?

The lights change to red just as they pull up in front of the shelter, and Polly feels the air in the car crackle with tension. Winifred turns in the front seat to see if Polly will do the right thing and ignore Buster, just as their mother has told her to.

Polly *tries* to do the right thing. She *wants* to do the right thing. But the rain is coming down harder now and Buster is right there, looking so damp and alone.

Polly keeps her gaze straight ahead, pretending not to notice him. But from the very corner of her eye, she can see he has spotted her. He jumps up and waves at her frantically. "Polly!" he calls, his voice filled with happiness.

"Polly! Over here! It's Buster!"

Her mother turns up the volume on the radio. An advertisement for a cauldron-cleaning potion blocks out Buster's yelling.

"Polly!" he shouts again, right at her window now, the rain wetting his fur. "Polly!"

Polly presses her lips together and her brow scrunches as she hears her best friend's voice turn from **happiness** to **confusion**.

"Polly?" he calls, more quietly this time.

But still she stares ahead, her heart **small** and **hurting**. Her mother looks approvingly at her.

A slow smile spreads over Winifred's face and she raises her eyebrows in disbelief. "Ha!" she says. "Who would have thought you could finally do something *right* for a change?"

Polly feels a deep **burn of shame** in her chest and her cheeks become hot. Her top lip curls and she glares at her sister. *The right thing for you might not be the right thing for me!* she thinks, and just as the lights change, Polly has an idea. Quickly, she draws a heart in her fogged-up window with a P at the top and a B at the bottom.

Through the scribbly lines she can just make out her best friend's smile as they pull away from the bus stop.

"Mom!" Winifred screeches. "Polly was writing notes to Buster!"

But Polly has already erased the drawing. "Was not!" she protests.

"Was too!" Winifred insists.

"Polly! Winifred! Stop it!" their mother shouts. "I'm trying to drive."

"Unbelievable!" Winifred sulks, crossing her arms and sliding down into the front seat. "You're *so* like your Aunt Hilda!" she adds, which is what their mother always says when one of them is driving her nuts.

"Winifred!" her mother scolds. "That's enough!"

Usually, being compared to Aunt Hilda really hurts Polly. Everyone knows Aunt Hilda was the most disobedient and rebellious witch in their town. And no child wants their mother to think of them as disobedient and rebellious.

But this time, as Polly gazes out her foggy car window at the dreary gray streets sliding past, she allows a small smile to creep across her lips. If being kind to your friends – even if they *are* monsters – is something Aunt Hilda would do, then perhaps being compared to her aunt isn't the worst thing in the world, after all?

Four

As Polly climbs out of the car at the school gate, her mother makes her promise to meet her back there at the end of the day. "Look after your sister!" she instructs Winifred as she drives off.

Winifred nods, but the moment the car is out of sight she runs into the playground. Polly doesn't mind. She has her *own* friends at school now! She hopes they are excited to see that she has returned.

Polly reaches her classroom just as the bell rings, but Miss Spinnaker is nowhere to be seen. Instead, old Mrs. Crabbe, their substitute teacher, is sitting at Miss Spinnaker's desk, putting her things away in the small tidy drawers.

"Where's Miss Spinnaker?" Polly pants, panic rising up through her belly. "I really need to talk to her!"

Mrs. Crabbe raises a thin eyebrow and **sneers** at Polly. "Good morning to you, too, Miss Proggett," she says, closing the last drawer with a thud. "I'm afraid Miss Spinnaker is no longer a teacher at Miss Madden's. The headmistress has decided to dismiss her."

"What?" says Polly. She can't believe what she is hearing. *Miss Spinnaker dismissed? That's impossible!* she thinks in dismay. *How could this have happened? Miss Spinnaker is the best teacher in the whole school!*

But then she glances at Mrs. Crabbe's jacket and sees a round yellow badge pinned there. On the badge is a crisp black *W. W* for Witch. Suddenly, Polly understands what has happened and she feels her chest fill with rage. Miss Spinnaker has been fired for being friendly with monsters!

Mrs. Crabbe pushes her
reading glasses down
her long pointy nose and
peers at Polly
over the top
of them.

"The word is *pardon*, Miss Proggett, and frankly, I'm surprised the headmistress didn't see fit to give *you* the same punishment for your role in this horrendous state of affairs. Then again, I suppose she thought it'd be better to keep an eye on you in the school grounds rather than have you gallivanting around town with that" – she sniffs – "*monster* friend of yours."

Polly feels her cheeks **burn hot**. *How dare Mrs. Crabbe talk about Buster like that! Buster is a hero!*

Her head **fizzes** and **spins**. This is not what she had expected on her first day back at school! Buster's medal ceremony canceled. Talk of war in Blackmoon Coven. And now

Miss Spinnaker fired from Miss Madden's? Everything is strange and unfair and Polly is too confused and angry to think straight.

As the students stream noisily into the room, she shoves her way back through them toward the doorway.

"Polly! Where are you going? Come back here this instant!" Mrs. Crabbe shrieks, trying to squeeze her large hips out from behind Miss Spinnaker's desk. "Sit down, Miss Proggett. Sit down! Catch that witch!" she screeches at the students, who are bumbling around her, confused by the commotion.

One hopeful warlock, Harold, always wanting to impress his teachers, dares to lay a hand on Polly's shoulder. Polly sees the W badge pinned to his sweater and feels a sudden heat flare in her chest. Sparks begin to flit around her fingertips.

"Oh. Sorry," he mumbles, and quickly drops his hand, stumbling backward down the corridor, eyes widening in alarm.

This time Polly doesn't bother trying to stop what's happening inside her. She is so angry now she couldn't stop it even if she wanted to.

A spell rolls up through her body and out of her fingertips ...

and a hot roaring wind pushes Harold and all the other straggling students back into the classroom, slamming the door behind them.

As Polly strides down the hallway toward the front entrance of the school, the hot wind continues to **whirl around her**, slamming shut all the classroom doors she passes, locking the students and teachers inside.

Blinking as she walks outside, Polly breathes deeply and tries to think. Her head is still fizzing from the spell, and she knows it won't be long before the head of Miss Madden's discovers what she's done. She dips her fingertips into her pocket and feels a slow warmth begin to creep up her hand.

Please tell me what to do! she begs the stones. *What can I do? Where can I go? Who can save this town if Miss Spinnaker is gone?*

She closes her eyes and the stones send the words **"SILVER WITCH"** into her thoughts. Her eyes snap open and suddenly Polly has the answer. Of course! Why didn't she think of it before? She knows what this town needs! A *true* Silver Witch, not a nine-year-old with a few magic stones in her pocket!

I'm sorry, Mom, she thinks as she walks through the neat gardens of Miss Madden's, away from the noise and confusion coming from inside the high stone walls. *But if I have another dangerous journey ahead, I am going to need a best friend by my side. And it certainly isn't anyone at Miss Madden's!*

She turns left at the front gates and begins the long walk up the steep cobbled road, toward the dark gloomy building at the top of Horrowful Hill.

Polly hopes with all her brave and fearful heart that it won't take long to find Buster. But she suspects that with everything that's been going on lately, witches may not be very welcome at Darklands School for Monsters.

Especially witches who are known for creating trouble.

Five

Polly slips through the tall iron gates and creeps across the Darklands grounds toward the main building. It is tall and imposing, very much in the style of the grand buildings of Polly's school, but with crumbling walls and cracked windows. Ivy grows in and out of the stones, and the paint on the enormous wooden doors is blistered and peeling.

Polly bends low and stays close to the building, so as not to be spotted by monsters idly staring out their classroom windows. She realizes she has no idea how she is going to find Buster, and wishes she'd had a better plan than just turning up at his school. She crouches down beside a tree and hopes a good idea might come to her.

Suddenly a bell rings. Polly's heart drops into her stomach. *It can't possibly be breaktime already?* she panics. But then she remembers Buster telling her that monsters have *five* break lunches a day. They get too hungry and too fidgety to concentrate on their schoolwork for more than an hour at a time.

Any moment now, five hundred hungry monsters will come hurtling outside. It's too late to make a run for it. She needs somewhere to hide! Polly grabs hold of the tree trunk to steady herself – and suddenly she knows what to do.

Polly may not be great at mixing potions and reading spells, but she is excellent at climbing trees. She never thought this could be a useful skill to have until now.

As a wave of monsters race into the playground, Polly yanks off her socks and shoes, tosses them into the bushes and quickly shimmies up the smooth, tall tree trunk. She hides herself as best she can in a scrawny bunch of leaves and peeks out at the monsters' playground, her heart leaping about in her chest. Polly searches for Buster's familiar green fur and white horns, but he is nowhere to be seen. *Please, Buster!* she thinks. *Where are you?*

Just then, Polly feels the branches underneath her sway. She looks down. There, squinting up at her, is a great big burly monster with hairy shoulders that make him look almost as broad as he is tall. His small yellow eyes widen as he spots Polly.

"No way!" he sneers. "Is that a *witch* up there?" His big purple lips curl back into a grin of disbelief.

Polly tries to climb a little higher, out of view, but the monster has already called his friends over. They surround the tree, cracking their knuckles and laughing. "A witch! A witch! A nasty little witch up there, spying on us! Come here, little witchy witch! Come down and play with us! We won't hurt you!"

The monsters **hoot** and **bellow** and smack each other's shoulders. Polly knows it will only be a moment before they climb up to grab her. She has no idea what they will do with her, but she really doesn't want to find out! She looks around to see if she can spot a teacher to rescue her, but none are in sight.

Polly knows there is only one way out

of there. She closes her eyes and breathes up a **HOT ANGRY SPELL** from her belly into her chest and down her arms to her fingertips. When she opens her eyes, the big hairy monster has already begun to climb toward her. She takes another deep breath and her fingers begin to **spark** and **crackle**. When the monster is close enough to reach out and grab her, she stares deep into his beady yellow eyes and scoops her arms up into the air.

"Leave. Me. Alone!" she roars, and the sparks shoot from her fingertips, blasting the monster out of the tree. Polly tries to grab hold of a branch to steady herself, but it is no use. She tumbles backward.

Down,
down,
down
she falls.

She squeezes her eyes shut and feels herself
land on the crowd of monsters below.

Six

"Polly!" comes a voice in her ear.

She can't believe what she is hearing. "Buster?" She snaps open her eyes.

"What are you doing here?" he yells, grabbing Polly from the grasp of another monster and tossing her onto his back.

"I had to find you!" Polly yelps. "They're saying there's going to be a war, Buster! Monsters against witches! We have to go and get help!"

They race across the schoolyard toward the main building. Buster begins to climb up one of its walls, Polly tucked under his arm. "I know," he pants. "Our teacher told us this morning. You shouldn't be here, Polly. It's too dangerous for you to be around monsters right now."

"Nothing we did made any difference," Polly despairs. "We thought everything would get better when we put the gorvan back to sleep, but somehow it's all gotten worse."

Polly looks down to see that the monsters from under the tree have followed them, and have started climbing up the wall. They're fast, and soon they have drawn level with Buster, who swings an arm out wide. He knocks back two of the monsters and they tumble to the ground, knocking the other three over in their fall. But as Buster reaches the roof of the grand building, the monsters on the ground begin to climb up the walls again. They **scrabble** and **scramble** among themselves to be first to reach the witch.

"Oi! Throw her down here!" the biggest one yells up to Buster, clearly thinking he is involved in their game.

Buster places Polly gently down on the rooftop. "I really wanted that medal, Polly. Mom and Dad would have been so proud," he sighs. "I would have been the first monster in Blackmoon Coven to ever get one!"

"And you need to get that medal so that all those silly witches out there can see that monsters can be good and brave, too!" Polly fumes.

"It's no use," says Buster, shaking his head, his eyes shiny with tears. "They'll never see it that way. Even you and I can't be friends anymore, Polly, can we? That's why you wouldn't look at me in the car this morning. My mom said I shouldn't go and visit you. She said your mom won't like it. The other witches on the street don't want us living there any longer, Polly. They tell Mom we should go and live on the other side of town where all the other monsters live." Buster shrinks in sadness. His fur turns a sickly gray.

"But that's ridiculous!" Polly says. "Monsters and witches should be able to live wherever they want. Everyone should be kind to each other, no matter *who* they are – witch *or* monster! That's what my dad used to tell me and Winifred." She sighs. "I wish he was still here. He would never have let something like this happen, I just know it."

Polly crawls to the edge of the building and peers over the side. The monsters are getting closer and closer.

"Buster, listen. I have to go and find my Aunt Hilda," Polly says as she crawls back over to him. "My dad's sister. Remember when we saw his ghost in the mines and he told me that she was the one who was supposed to have the magic stones? I have to find her, and persuade her to come back and help us. The stones told me Blackmoon Coven needs a Silver Witch to stop this war, and she's a *real* Silver Witch. Not just a kid, like me!" She stands up and takes his paw in her hands. "Will you come with me and help me find my Aunt Hilda? Please?"

"Oh, Polly, I don't know if I can," Buster says, scratching his horns. "My mom's still cross with me for running away last time!"

"Please, Buster! I can't do this without you. Aunt Hilda will stop this war. And then you can have your medal ceremony, like you're meant to!"

"Do you really think so?" Buster asks hopefully. A small smile twitches in the corner of his mouth and he begins to **expand a little** with happiness. "Do you really think I'll still be able to get my medal?"

"Yes, of course!" Polly promises him.

"And the ceremony with the afternoon tea and we all get to dress up and eat cake afterward?" Buster says, his cheeks turning pink.

"Yes, Buster! As much cake as you want," Polly says patiently. She glances toward the edge of the rooftop and sees a monster's paw appear. "But first we've got to a find a way out of here!"

Seven

Buster puts his paw on Polly's shoulder. "Sing to me," he says. His fur is bright green again.

"What?" says Polly. She looks across nervously as a monster's head pops up over the edge of the building.

"Sing to me. Our happy song," he grins.

"Is this really the best time?" cries Polly. But then suddenly she understands. "Oh!"

She smiles and takes a deep breath. Her voice comes out trembly at first, but then grows stronger and stronger.

"Me and you, you and me.
That's the way it will always be."

Buster closes his eyes. He grows and grows. Polly clings to his fur as he grows bigger and lighter, until soon they are bobbing in the cloudy gray sky. The school, the grounds and the swarm of confused and angry monsters become smaller and smaller beneath them.

Polly and Buster float over the rooftops of Blackmoon Coven. Polly doesn't stop singing, even when her throat begins to feel hoarse. As they float, she looks down at the town. How quickly it has changed from the place she knew and loved to a place of suspicion and fear.

Polly spies her favorite sweetshop below, where she and her sister buy sparkpoppers that turn their tongues blue. Next to it is the shop where her mother has her cauldron cleaned, and the store that sells enormous monster shoes is nearby. But all of them are closed; monsters and witches are hiding in their houses, warily peering through curtains.

Even the once-busy marketplace has only a few stalls that remain open; monsters on one side and witches on the other. *Perhaps Aunt*

Hilda was right to leave this town all those years ago? Polly thinks sadly as she sings, clinging to Buster's fur, high up in the sky. *Who could live in a place where no one trusts anyone anymore?*

In the distance, she sees the Central Patrol hovering on their broomsticks. They are the Mayor's team of witches who guard Blackmoon Coven and keep order in the streets. The sight of them out in full force, watching out for any invading monster gangs, makes Polly feel sadder still.

"Polly?" says Buster quietly when her voice has begun to croak. "I'm going to need to land soon." She can feel him shrink with tiredness as the happy feeling from the song begins to wear off.

Polly looks down again. They are drifting over tightly packed rows of small, shabby houses. Polly knows this is the monsters' side of town. "Oh, Buster, I don't think it's safe here!" she says, but she can feel Buster shrinking even more. "Can you hold on a bit longer?" Polly pleads, but he shakes his head and Polly can hear his tummy rumble. She knows he will be hungry, and this definitely doesn't make him happy.

They begin to drop to the ground.

"Wait!" says Polly. She dips her fingers into her pocket and closes her eyes for a second to ask the stones to guide them somewhere safe. She sees a tall shinnaker tree appear in her mind and when she opens her eyes again, it is right in front of them. "There!" says Polly, pointing to the tree, and Buster breathes out in relief.

Buster lands gracefully on the topmost branches just as he shrinks back to his normal size. He swings down through the tree with Polly tucked under one arm, landing in the tiny garden below with a gentle thud. They sit with their backs against the rough bark for a moment, exhausted from their flight across town. Polly hopes desperately that the stones have led them somewhere safe.

The roots of the tall tree take up almost all the yard and have buckled the narrow pathway that leads to a wide wooden porch. As they watch, the back door swings open and a large ginger-haired, green-eyed monster pokes her head out, her mouth dropping in surprise.

Buster quickly stands up to hide Polly, but it is too late.

"Is that a *witch* in my garden?" the monster shouts. A little monster looks out from behind her knees and **squeals** in fear.

"Quick!" says Buster, lifting Polly up onto his shoulders. "We'd better go!"

The monster peers at them more closely and suddenly claps a paw over her mouth. "Oh! You're that witch who was on the news just now." Then she looks at Buster. "And you're her friend!"

Polly can't believe what she is hearing. The *news*?

The monster steps back into the house. "Come along, Deeble," she says to her son, who peers up at her fearfully. "These two are trouble!"

"Wait!" Polly says, suddenly understanding why the stones sent her here. She jumps down off Buster's shoulders and rushes up to the back door before the monster can close it. "Is that your son's name? *Deeble*? As in Deeble *Dombleby*?"

The monster narrows her eyes. "Who told you that?"

Polly takes a deep breath and feels a little bloom of hope unfurl inside her chest. "Was your husband also called Deeble Dombleby?"

The monster's brow creases. "Yes," she says warily. "How do you know my husband?"

"My dad was Samuel Proggett," Polly says gently. "Your husband worked with my father. In the mines."

"Oh," says the monster, her voice becoming very quiet and sad. She swings her child up onto her hip and gazes at Polly, her eyes softening. "Well, I heard Sammy Proggett had daughters, but I never expected to see one turn up on my back doorstep!" She sighs and shakes her big shaggy head. "What strange times these are. Well, come in, child! Any family of Sam Proggett is always welcome in the Dombleby home."

Polly turns around and beckons for Buster, who scratches his horns in bewilderment.

They step into the monster's small, tidy kitchen, where the television is still blaring in the background. In the corner of the room is a huge fireplace, with a worn floral armchair in front of it. A colorful ball of wool and a half-knitted sweater lie discarded in a wicker basket, which is also filled with toy trucks carved out of moonwood and a stuffed felt goblin. The kitchen smells like fresh baked chipperty bread and wet woolen socks.

The monster places her little one onto the floor and he runs out of the room. Polly and Buster sit at the big wooden table to watch the rest of the news while the monster attaches a kettle to a big iron hook above the coals.

"*... We are live at Miss Madden's Academy of Witches and Warlocks, where it appears a spell done by student Polly Proggett has gone horribly wrong,*" the reporter says.

Polly's stomach drops. Is that really *her* they are talking about?

Buster snorts with laughter as a shot of a classroom filled with toads appears on the screen. "What? Is Miss Madden's a school for *toads*, now?" He laughs loudly at his own joke.

Then he stops and looks at Polly, his expression changing from amusement to shock, then disbelief. "No! You didn't?"

Polly's eyes are fixed to the screen. A horrible feeling comes over her. She couldn't have, could she? It's true she didn't look behind any of those doors once they slammed shut, but surely her spell wasn't *that* powerful?

Then the furious face of her headmistress comes into view.

"All of grades four, five and six," she fumes. "Every student *and* teacher turned into toads. It's going to take me *days* to mix up enough potion to turn them all back again."

The camera zooms in on the headmistress's terrifying eyes, just as a toad leaps onto her shoulder. She brushes it away in disgust. "Polly Proggett, if you are listening, you can be very sure you won't get away with this. Very, *very* sure."

Buster stares at Polly, his eyes wide, his paw clapped over his mouth.

"Buster! It's not funny!" Polly says, glaring at him. "I am in so much trouble! Mom will *never* forgive me!"

"Oh," says Buster, swallowing back a giggle. "That's bad. That's really bad." But his eyebrows jiggle like two squirming caterpillars.

"Tea?" says the ginger-haired monster,

carrying over a tray with a steaming teapot and a big slice of cake for each of them. "I find that tea and cake usually fixes most problems. Wouldn't you agree?"

"Definitely!" says Buster, reaching for the biggest piece of cake, his stomach **roaring with happiness**. "Oh yes, most definitely."

Eight

"Now, what brings you to my doorstep?" Mrs. Dombleby says, taking off her apron and sitting down on a big wooden chair beside Polly.

Polly picks at the orange-and-yellow cake and puts some in her mouth. It really is delicious. *How is it that monster food always tastes so much better than witch food?* she wonders, remembering her mother's **disgusting homemade jackarons.** She hopes her mother has been too busy at work to see the news. Polly has no idea how she is going to explain *this* mess!

"And some tea," Mrs. Dombleby encourages, pushing the cup toward Polly, who lifts it obligingly to her lips. She takes a sip and is surprised at the way it **fizzes** fruitily in her mouth. "You too," the monster tells Buster, who has almost finished his cake.

He takes a big gulp of tea and grins at them both happily.

"Well, it's kind of hard to explain," Polly murmurs. "And you might find some of it hard to believe …"

"Try me," says Mrs. Dombleby kindly, refilling Polly's teacup and nudging it toward her.

Polly takes a deep breath. She is considering what she can tell the monster when she finds the words tumbling straight from her lips, almost as if she can't control them.

Polly tells Mrs. Dombleby about Miss Spinnaker, and being a Silver Witch, and the stones from her father. She tells the story of how they sent her into the Hollow Valley mines, where she found the ghosts of her father and the other miners, who'd trapped the gorvan and stayed behind to stop it escaping into Blackmoon Coven.

"A gorvan?" Mrs. Dombleby's eyes widen.

"Yes!" says Polly, looking up into the monster's worried face. "But they weren't able to put it to sleep," Polly continues. "It would have escaped out of the mines, but my father managed to trap it with his final spell before he died. That's why its purple mist has been seeping out into our town all these last years and turning things bad," Polly sighs deeply. "So when I was in the mines I did the spell to put the gorvan back to sleep so all the ghosts could finally rest, and the witches and monsters of Blackmoon Coven could be at peace again."

"She was so brave!" Buster interrupts, glowing a little with pride.

"But it didn't work!" Polly says to Buster. "Witches and monsters still hate each other ..."

Suddenly she realizes she's let her secret out.

"But please, **please**, **please**, you can't tell anyone what I did!" Polly begs Mrs. Dombleby. "We're not allowed to do spells out of school and I've already been caught doing two. If the headmistress finds out I did a third one, I'll be expelled from Miss Madden's." Polly groans. "But I'll probably be expelled now anyway ..." she says, picturing the furious face of her headmistress on the news. She hangs her head, and then looks up at Mrs. Dombleby, who has tears spilling down her furry cheeks.

"You really saw my husband in there?" she croaks, taking Polly's little hand in her big rough paws.

Polly nods, remembering the skinny ghost monster with the big teeth who introduced himself as Deeble. "He told me to tell you he loves you and he hopes you named the baby after him," Polly adds in a whisper, surprised that she remembered this last important detail without the note she had written down.

Big sobs burst from Mrs. Dombleby's chest. She stands up and wraps her furry arms tightly around Polly and cries into her hair. "I did!" she sobs, loudly. "I did name our baby Deeble. You saw 'im. That was our little Deeble Junior right there!"

Polly sits still, feeling her heart ache. Even Buster's eyes have filled with fat, shimmering tears and he slows his chewing down to a more respectful rate.

Eventually Mrs. Dombleby stops crying. She blows her nose loudly on a big spotted handkerchief. Then she sits down beside Polly again, her cheeks wet and shiny. "Thank you," she says. "Not just for the message from my Deeble, but for telling me your whole story. That was a brave thing to do."

"I wasn't sure you'd believe me," Polly offers quietly. "Not many grown-ups believe stories about ghosts and gorvans."

"Maybe not many grown-up *witches* would believe you," the monster says, "but I do. Most monsters believe in gorvans." Mrs. Dombleby dabs at her red nose and glances down at the teapot. "I knew you'd tell me the truth, anyway. You might be surprised to hear this, but I actually know your Miss Spinnaker," she says. "She was one of them nice witches who weren't rude to us monsters. Treated us with respect. She used to come to my cake stall at the market and I'd swap my cakes for herbs from her garden to make tea with." A smile plays on the corner of the monster's lips and she pats the teapot with a big ginger paw. "Some of them herbs she gave me may have been, um … let's just say, *magical*."

Polly gasps. "No way! I thought that tea tasted funny! That was truth tea, wasn't it?"

Buster sticks out his tongue in alarm. Polly sees the little sparkles on the end of it.

"But that's not allowed!" Polly protests. "You're not supposed to give a magic tea to someone without warning them first!"

"Well, I weren't going to invite a *dangerous* witch into my home without knowing if you were telling the truth now, was I?" the monster says, **smiling mischievously.** "But now I know I can trust you. My name's Milly. Friends?" she says, holding out her paw for Polly to shake.

Polly smiles and takes Milly's paw. "Friends," she agrees.

Buster grins sheepishly. "Um, now that we are friends," he says, playing with the crumbs on his plate, "I wonder if I could ask you something, Milly?"

"Of course," Milly says, smiling warmly.

"Well, it's a bit embarrassing," Buster says, his cheeks glowing pink.

"What is it, love?" Milly says, taking his paw. "Come on now, don't be shy."

"Um," Buster glances up at Polly, then back to Milly again. "Um, do you think I could have a little more cake? I'm starving!"

"Buster!" Polly says, glaring at him.

Milly laughs uproariously. "He has quite an appetite, this one, doesn't he?" she says to Polly.

"You have no idea!" says Polly, rolling her eyes.

Nine

"So what are you doing all the way over on *this* side of town?" Milly asks, as they watch Buster gobble up another huge slice of monster cake. Deeble Junior has ventured back into the kitchen and climbed up onto his mother's lap, a knitted toy monster in his paw. He still peers at Polly suspiciously, but Buster makes him laugh.

"I ran away from school," Polly explains, feeling her cheeks heat up. "Mom will be so cross with me, but I didn't know what else to do." She sighs. "I thought putting the gorvan back to sleep would make everything go back to how it was before. I know witches and monsters haven't always gotten along, but at least they weren't talking about starting a war!"

Milly smiles kindly at Polly. "A lot of us are angry, my sweets. But anger isn't always a bad thing. Anger can be used to start a war. But it can also be used to start a revolution."

"That's why we need to find my Aunt Hilda," Polly says firmly. "Dad told me she would have been the most powerful Silver Witch

Blackmoon Coven had ever known if she hadn't run away. She'll save us!"

"That's the spirit!" Milly says. "She sounds amazing!"

"She is!" Polly says proudly. "When Dad was still alive she used to send him postcards from all over the world." Polly smiles fondly, remembering her dad tucking her and Winifred into bed at night and telling them all about their Aunt Hilda's wild adventures. "One time he told us she lived underground with a tribe of goblins and only ate grass and insects for a whole year. Another time she rode a real live dragon!" She sighs. "Dad said she's not afraid of anything. I can't wait to meet her!"

"Well, it sounds like Blackmoon Coven could certainly do with someone as fearless as she is," says Milly. "But how are you going to find her?"

Polly picks the grubby purple pouch up off the table. "These will tell me," she says, tipping the three little stones into her palm, where they *gleam* expectantly. "I just hope it's not too far away."

"Me too!" grimaces Buster. "My mom will be cross if I'm not home for dinner."

Polly closes her fingers over the stones. Then she takes a deep breath and squeezes her eyes shut. A **warm ball of air** opens in her chest like a sunflower. It flows into her shoulders, along her arms, right down to her fingertips.

Polly feels the
smoothness of the
stones in her palm,
and soon they
begin to warm.

Where is Aunt Hilda? she asks them and within moments, the visions unfurl in her mind. She sees rolling green hills, fields of ripening bley and a small village tucked into a sunny valley. It's full of crumbling white stone buildings and little cobbled streets. On the edge of the village is a dear little farm and a wooden house with a verandah wrapped around it.

Aunt Hilda? Polly asks again, and she sees a vision of a witch's face with eyes just like her father's. *There you are!* says Polly in her mind. And as she has this thought, Aunt Hilda's smile falters for a moment and her eyes narrow, as if she is trying to see something very far away. *Aunt Hilda, we need your help!* Polly tells her.

I know you can hear me. Please show us how to find you.

"Well?" says Buster, when Polly opens her eyes again.

Polly lets her mind clear and the heat in her chest die down. The stones stay warm in her palm. "Well, the good news is that she's actually not too far away!" she says brightly. "She's in a little village just north of Blackmoon Coven. Past the mines and the Amber Skull Forest." She can't help but feel a little worm of disappointment turn in her belly. If her aunt had been living so close all this time, why had she never once thought to visit? Polly shakes the idea from her mind. *She must be busy doing something terribly important,* she reassures herself. *After all, Aunt Hilda is a very powerful Silver Witch.*

"Ooh dear," Milly says, looking anxious. "It's not safe to be traveling through the woods these days. Not with the Amber Skull Forest Gang roaming about."

"Actually, I wasn't thinking of traveling *through* the forest..." Polly smiles apologetically at Buster.

Buster groans, dropping his forehead onto the table. "You're going to make me get on a broomstick again, aren't you?"

Polly grins and nods. "The stones also told me you might have a broomstick we could borrow, Milly?" she says, remembering the last little image that had flitted through her mind.

"I do!" Milly says, her eyebrows shooting up. "My word, those stones are good. I have an old one that a witch gave me, but I'm not sure how to work it. You can keep it if you can get it going. I'll fetch it for you." She stands up, and swings Deeble Junior onto her hip again. "Are you scared of flying, dear?"

Buster tries to make his mouth say "no," but a "yes" sneaks out instead. "Blooming truth tea!" he grumbles.

"No harm in being scared of heights," Milly says as she opens a tall narrow cupboard and pulls an old-fashioned broomstick out from behind some mops and buckets.

"It's not the *height*, it's the *speed*." Buster frowns, rubbing his tummy. "I just get airsick, that's all."

Polly giggles. "Good thing you only had two servings of cake then, isn't it?" She takes the broomstick from Milly and turns it over in her hands. "Thanks, Milly!" Polly smiles at Buster, who has shrunk a little at the prospect of getting on a broomstick again. "This will be perfect for the two of us. Lucky we found you!"

Milly smiles at Polly. "My Deeble only had good words to say about working with your da, my love. As far as I'm concerned, any child of

Sam Proggett can only be a good witch!" She wipes a tear from her eye with a speckled paw.

Polly feels her heart **bloom** and sends a little thank you in her mind to her dad, who still makes her proud.

Just at that moment a news flash appears on the television and Milly turns the sound up.

"Latest reports from the Mayor's Central Patrol have come in!" barks the broadcaster. *"There have been sightings of the Amber Skull Forest Gang on the outskirts of town. All witches are advised to stay indoors. I repeat, all witches are advised to stay indoors!"*

"Come on!" Polly says, grabbing Buster's paw. "We need to hurry!"

"You go and find that aunt of yours and bring her back to fix this mess," Milly calls after them, shoving a cloth bag into Polly's hands as they run into her backyard. "Tell her to hurry up so we can all go back to living peacefully, you hear?"

"I will!" promises Polly and she twists the tip of the broomstick until it sputters to a start. In no time at all, she is flying over Blackmoon Coven again, the wind in her hair, the magic stones in her pocket and a bag full of monster cake bouncing against her hip.

But most important of all, Polly has her Buster, holding on tightly behind her, breathing nervously into her ear. Even though she knows he would have been much happier climbing the play equipment at Darklands, or even sitting at Milly's table eating cake and watching TV, here he is, on the back of her broomstick, brave and true.

She smiles gratefully. Nothing ever feels impossible with a best friend by your side.

Ten

When Polly and Buster reach the Amber Skull Forest, Polly takes the broomstick as high as she dares so she can't be spotted by the monster gang below. Far beneath them, she can just make out the little clearing where she knows their headquarters are hidden. She shivers. How many monsters are gathered down there now, planning to attack Blackmoon Coven?

Milly had told them the Amber Skull Forest Gang had been roaming monster neighborhoods at night, hoping to recruit more members. And the news had reported more witches signing up to join the Mayor's Central Patrol.

Polly thinks back to dear Miss Spinnaker, who had tried her hardest to convince Carmen, her old friend and the leader of the monster gang, to try to sort things out with Mayor Redwolf. And where did that get her? Fired from her job at Miss Madden's for being a friend to monsters! Polly wonders where she is now.

Don't worry, Miss Spinnaker! she thinks. *My aunt will fix all of this and you will be able to get your job back. And Buster will get his medal. And everyone will live peacefully again. The stones told me a Silver Witch will fix all this and as you told me yourself: the stones don't lie!*

When the sun shifts higher in the sky, they pause to eat the rest of Milly's cake for lunch and drink gritty water from a creek. Polly wishes she had packed better for the journey, or thought to bring a cloak to keep herself warm. The clouds let through a little streak of sunlight every now and then, but the wind is biting and cold.

At least the stones help keep Polly on track. If she begins to stray in the wrong direction, they quickly heat up in her pocket. She corrects the angle of her broomstick and they cool to their regular temperature, reassuring her, guiding her, reminding her she is not alone.

Buster breathes into the back of her neck, his arms still wrapped tightly around her waist, but she notices his breathing has become calmer. Every now and then she even hears him humming to himself. Polly knows traveling on the back of a broomstick will never be his favorite thing, but she is glad he is starting to relax a little.

Then, in the distance, Polly spots a shimmering cloud of rainbow. It swirls and twists into a snake-thin line, then rolls around itself like a snail shell, glittering brightly against the dull gray sky before easing out into a wispy cloud again. She leans forward to get a better view and blinks twice.

It can't be! she thinks, but as they approach Polly feels her heart **squeeze with delight.** She has heard witches talk of this marvel before, but never in her wildest dreams did she think she might be lucky enough to experience it herself.

"Buster!" she breathes in disbelief. "I think … I think we're about to pass through a swarm of musical Bellfaeries!"

"What?" says Buster, peeking over her shoulder. He gasps when he spies what Polly has seen. "No way!"

"Yes way!" says Polly, laughing as they hear the sound of a thousand tiny voices, high

and tinkling like bells. "Try to catch one!" she
urges Buster. "We're going to fly right through
them!"

"Oh, I don't know!" Buster says nervously, and she feels him bury his face between her shoulder blades as they pass through the swarm of tiny creatures. The Bellfaeries, as small and fast as bumblebees, spin around them, bouncing off their bodies and tugging at Polly's hair.

Polly quickly protects her eyes with one hand and pins her lips tight so as not to accidentally swallow one. Buster grips her tighter and she squints into the cloud of thousands of tiny colorful bodies, concentrating hard to keep the broomstick from spinning out of control. Within seconds, the cloud begins to thin. Polly tries to catch one as they zip past, but she is much too slow.

"Ooh, here's one!" Buster says, gently pulling a Bellfaery out of Polly's hair.

"Quick! Make a wish," Polly says, "then pass it to me!" But before she has even finished her sentence, Buster yelps in pain.

Polly roars with laughter. "Did it bite you?"

"Yes!" Buster shouts, shaking his paw. "I really don't like those things!"

"Don't you know how rare it is to see a real live cloud of *Bellfaeries?*" Polly says. "If you catch one, you can make a wish!"

"The only thing I wish is never to run into a silly cloud of Bellfaeries again!" Buster grumbles, sucking his paw. "And that we could finish this blooming broomstick ride!"

"Seriously?" Polly giggles. "Not peace in Blackmoon Coven?"

"OK, OK, peace in Blackmoon Coven," Buster agrees. "But only if it meant I never had to ride on a broomstick again!"

Polly smiles and flies on, dreamily imagining all the things she would have wished for. Peace in Blackmoon Coven would be top of the list, of course. But she wouldn't turn down one of those fancy new **BROOMSTICK 500s**. Or a pair of **SUPER TRANSPORT SHOES**. In royal purple! Three taps of their heels and you can be anywhere you want within the blink of an eye.

Eventually, Buster's voice pulls her out of her daydreaming.

"Are we there yet?" he asks for the hundredth time, and this time, when Polly touches the stones, they say: *Yes! Yes you are!*

Polly looks down in delight to see they are flying over the little village she saw in her visions. And there, in a sun-drenched valley, is the wooden house with the wraparound verandah.

"Aunt Hilda!" Polly murmurs. "We're here!"

As if she had been expecting them, Polly sees a tall, dark-haired witch open the door and step out onto the verandah.

"Is that her?" she hears Buster ask, close to her ear.

"I think so," says Polly, her stomach curling with **excitement**. But then she sees something she *definitely* hadn't expected: a scraggly stream of barefooted children running past the witch, squealing and whooping into the sunshine.

Polly hears Buster gasp. "Polly!" he says, his voice rising to a squeak. "Can you see what I see?"

Polly feels her heart **butterfly** in her chest. There, playing in Aunt Hilda's front garden, are a dozen or so children.

Children of all shapes and sizes.

Children of witches *and* monsters.

Eleven

Polly circles the house for a few moments, unsure of whether to land or to wait until everyone returns inside. Eventually, Aunt Hilda lifts her gaze from the children she is supervising, and calls out, "You may as well come down!"

Polly feels uncomfortable. She had thought her reunion with her aunt would be just the two of them, and somehow special and sacred.

Now that this plan has been ruined, she feels **anXious** and **prickly**. But she takes a deep breath and obediently tips the broomstick handle downward.

As soon as they touch the ground, they are surrounded by a swarm of children, eyes and mouths wide. The little ones reach out their sticky fingers and paws to touch the smooth wooden handle, gasping loudly in amazement, and the older ones hover behind them, staring openly at Polly and Buster.

"What?" Polly frowns irritably. "Don't tell me you've never seen a kid ride a broomstick before?"

"They've never seen a *broomstick* before," Aunt Hilda says, smiling, as she glides up behind them. "We don't use them out here. All right, children," she says. "That's enough disruption for one day. Back inside and you can all work on your science projects until I get there. No explosions, though. Go on! Off you go!"

The children amble off reluctantly, turning to stare at Polly and Buster, and whispering among themselves.

"Well," says Aunt Hilda. "This is not something you see every day. What are you two doing here? Are you lost?" She runs both hands through her dark wavy hair, flecked with glimmers of white and silver, and twists it into a loose bun at the nape of her neck. It immediately comes undone and tumbles down her back again.

Up close, Polly notices Aunt Hilda's arms are tanned and covered in inky drawings. Polly tries not to stare at them, but she is fascinated. She has seen drawings like this on smooth-skinned monsters and the odd muscly warlock, but never on a tall, slender witch like Aunt Hilda. Her blue stripy shirt, rolled up at the sleeves, is faded and worn, and her pants are patched at the knees. In her left nostril glints a tiny silver stud in the shape of a crescent moon.

"No, we're … we're not lost," stammers Polly, looking up into the witch's dark honey-colored eyes, which are thickly outlined in black. They are the exact same color as her father's, but deeply creased at the edges from smiling.

"We came to find *you*. Your brother is my dad. I mean …" she corrects herself, shaking her head. "I mean *was*." She takes a deep breath to calm herself and tries again. "Aunt Hilda. It's me! It's your niece, Polly."

The witch frowns and peers down at Polly. Then she brings her face in closer to look deep into Polly's eyes. Her hair smells like wood smoke and nettles. "You're *Sam's* kid? Sam had a *kid*? No way!" She claps her hand over her mouth.

"Two, actually," Buster offers.

"*You're* Sam's kid, too?" Aunt Hilda says.

Buster snorts with laughter.

"No, I have an older sister," Polly explains. "Buster's my *friend*."

Polly watches carefully to see if her aunt will make a face, but her aunt doesn't seem to notice. She is still staring at Polly in amazement, like she can't quite believe her eyes.

"My big brother had a baby," she murmurs. "*Two* babies! Oh, tumbling toadstools. I'm an *aunt*!" She claps both hands to her chest like her heart might burst out of there at any moment. "Oh wow! You look like him, too. How old are you, darling? Eight? Nine? What's your name again?"

"Polly," says Polly. "And I'm nine." She is pleased her aunt has guessed correctly. Most grown-ups have no idea about kids' ages and guess the most ridiculous things.

"Oh, moping moonbeams!

Who would've thought this day would ever come?" Aunt Hilda laughs, her eyes shiny with happy tears. She grabs Polly into her arms and squeezes her tight.

Polly's heart **soars.** She closes her eyes for a second and can almost remember being hugged like this by her father.

Hilda pulls away and grins at Polly. "Oh my lordy lord. My big brother's littlest kid. Well, you'd better come inside and meet *my* children." She smiles warmly at Buster and holds out a hand to each of them.

"They're your *children*?" Polly says, unable to hide her surprise.

"Well, they're not exactly *mine*, obviously," Aunt Hilda chuckles. "I just mind them while their parents are at work. The older ones help out on the farm when they've finished their book learning for the day, seeding the pilly-pillys and milking the goopins. That sort of thing."

"Witches *and* monsters?" Polly asks in disbelief.

"Yes, darling. Witches *and* monsters," Aunt Hilda says knowingly. "I can see Blackmoon Coven hasn't improved much since I left. We have lots to catch up on. But first, you two must be hungry after traveling such a long way?"

"Oh, yes!" Buster sighs. "Starving!"

Polly elbows him in the ribs and hisses, "We just ate, Buster!"

"Good!" Aunt Hilda says. "Because we have jamcakes in the oven. They're a bit of a specialty in our house. I hope you like jamcakes?"

Buster nearly falls over himself with excitement. "They're my absolute most bestest favorite," he swoons and follows Aunt Hilda into the house, his tummy rumbling loudly.

Twelve

The smell of jamcakes makes Polly's mouth prickle as they enter the sunny kitchen behind Aunt Hilda. Rickety wooden chairs surround a long table laid with a red-and-white-checked tablecloth, and there is a speckled jug of yellow clawflowers in the middle.

"Teatime!" Aunt Hilda calls, and all the children rollick into the kitchen.

A monster drags in two extra seats from the hallway, and Polly and Buster sit down to a feast of jamcakes and bilberries, and fresh milk from Aunt Hilda's goopin herd. Polly has never drunk fresh goopin milk before. It is still warm and frothy and smells ever so slightly of goopin dung, but it is delicious. So are the jamcakes, hot and sticky, straight from the oven.

The children chatter noisily among themselves. Polly realizes they must assume she and Buster are just two new children who have arrived to join Aunt Hilda's clan.

Eventually, when everyone has eaten and the cleaning up has been done, the big children carry the little children out to the nap room, and tuck them under lumpy hand-knitted blankets to sleep. Then they wander outside to play in the garden.

Buster joins a game of hide-and-seek and Aunt Hilda beckons Polly to sit beside her on the porch on a wicker sofa full of faded floral cushions. She plops a fat black-and-white cat onto the ground to make room for Polly. It slinks off, glaring at them before it disappears under the house.

"Finally!" her aunt smiles, smoothing Polly's hair with one big freckled hand and cradling a mug of lavender tea in the other. "A little moment to ourselves, hey? Tell me about your family, and your life, and everything that's been going on in Blackmoon Coven since I've been gone."

So Polly tells Aunt Hilda everything. She is not sure if she will believe the story about the ghosts and the gorvan in the mines, but Aunt Hilda listens without batting an eyelid. Polly wonders if she is still a little affected by Milly's truth tea, she's talking so freely with this aunt who she has never met, but she suspects it's more that Aunt Hilda makes her feel safe. There is something about Aunt Hilda that feels familiar, like trees and earth and things you can rely on. And she is relieved to discover that Aunt Hilda already knows about the accident in the Hollow Valley mines.

"I always suspected there was a gorvan in those mines, but no one wanted to believe me," Aunt Hilda says sadly. "I wish my brother had never taken that job. He would have made a wonderful painter if our parents had only let him. So sad. Such a waste." She shakes her head.

A painter! Polly thinks. *I never knew that!* And she wonders how many other things about her father she doesn't know, and now never will. She wonders also if Aunt Hilda ever considered coming back for her father's funeral. She knows her mother was hurt that her aunt never came, but she feels too shy to ask.

Polly gazes at her aunt's sharp profile and fiery dark eyes in awe and admiration as she tells Polly stories of traveling the world. Of rolling purple valleys where wild unicorns roam, dense floating cities inhabited by water sprites and winding underground caves full of goblins, whose earth magic is far more powerful than any magic a Black Witch could hope to conjure.

"You have no idea how amazing the world is out there, my darling," her aunt continues, "and … check this out!" She pushes her sleeve higher up her arm to show off more of her inky drawings. "A tattoo for every place I've been!" she says proudly. "Some of them I did myself." She runs her short dark fingernails over a drawing with wobblier lines than the others.

"They're the ones that aren't quite so brilliant," she chuckles. "But there's an awesome one on my back! I'll show you later, if you like? A big scaly dragon I had done in the city of Gormanstan, deep in the winter gorges."

Polly gazes at her aunt's strong brown forearms covered in drawings and tries to picture all the places she has been to. She can't imagine anything more daring than traveling the world on her own. Polly has decided that despite what her mother would say, being compared to Aunt Hilda is a very fine thing indeed!

"Why did you decide to stay here, if you've been to so many amazing places?" Polly asks. "I mean, it's kind of pretty, but it's very … quiet?"

Polly was almost going to say "boring," but catches herself just in time. All the same, when she looks around at Aunt Hilda's simple home, she can't really understand why such a powerful and adventurous witch would choose to live here.

"I don't know," Aunt Hilda says, shrugging. "I arrived here six years ago and just fell in love with the place. Everyone here is kind, and it didn't take long before I found myself minding all the kids while their parents went out to work in the fields each day. And now I teach them to count and read in return for food and clothing. So I guess I'm almost like their teacher!" Aunt Hilda laughs.

Polly shivers when she hears how similar her aunt's laugh is to her memory of her father's.

"Which is funny, isn't it?" Aunt Hilda continues, not noticing Polly's reaction. "Because I hated school. I had friends at Miss Madden's, of course. But there's probably only one of them I was sorry to leave ..." Her eyes glaze over a little as she thinks back to her school days. Then she tosses her head, snapping out of her trance. "But I can tell you, Polly, I learned more in my travels than I did at Miss Madden's! School never really worked for me. All those rules and writing in straight lines. I'd *never* make kids do that." She rolls her eyes. "And all that keeping quiet! Boring as bat skulls!"

She stops to call out to a couple of monsters who are climbing a tree. "Pumpy! Dooper! What in canny cauldrons makes you think those skinny little branches would be strong enough to hold two great big monsters like you, huh?"

She chuckles fondly as the monsters climb back down again. Polly feels a tiny flame of jealousy spark inside her. Her aunt is so clever and so amazing, and these kids have had her watch over them for six years. Even though she's *Polly's* aunt, not theirs.

"I suppose the whole time I was traveling, I was looking for somewhere to call home. A place where everyone could get along." Her aunt smiles, gazing out over her tidy vegetable patch toward the distant fields of goldening bley. "And I found it, right here."

"But don't you ever miss Blackmoon Coven?" Polly asks, hopefully.

"**Pfft!**" Aunt Hilda sniffs. "Not at all. It's a horrible place, if you ask me. All that hatred between witches and monsters. Your dad and I were always getting into trouble for hanging out with monsters when we were little."

Polly smiles. *Just like me!* she thinks.

"Look!" her aunt says, pointing out into the garden, where the children are playing happily. "Can you see any difference between them? No, of course you can't! Children are children and they don't care if you are a witch or a warlock or a monster, so why should grown-ups care? In this town you can live as you want and love who you want. And that's fine by me." She takes a big gulp of tea and pats Polly's knee, before calling out to two of the younger witches to be gentle with her seedlings.

"You *can* still do magic though, right?" Polly asks, feeling suddenly nervous. "I mean, you *were* born a Silver Witch? That's what Dad said." She realizes she hasn't seen any signs of magic since they arrived. In fact, Aunt Hilda's life looks remarkably ordinary!

Aunt Hilda checks that no one is looking. Then she tips her mug in Polly's direction and

waves her fingers over it. Polly peers into the
mug and sees it has become filled with pearls.
She gasps. Aunt Hilda waves her hand again
and the pearls turn into snails. Then she clicks
her fingers and the mug is filled with tea again.

She winks at Polly. "Only for fun and only when no one is looking. Witches and warlocks don't learn magic here because they believe in equality between all species. As soon as you teach witches magic it gives them too much power. It's not fair on the monsters. Look at what's happened in Blackmoon Coven! I'd never let that happen here!"

Polly sinks back into the sofa.

The stones were right, she thinks, relieved. *They said it would take a Silver Witch to fix the problems of Blackmoon Coven. And Aunt Hilda is exactly the right one!*

Suddenly she remembers that time is slipping away from them. Who knows what terrible things have been happening back home while she and Aunt Hilda have been sitting on her back porch sipping tea?

Polly decides she can't wait any longer to ask ...

Thirteen

"No, no and no!" Aunt Hilda says, as she stands by the stove stirring soup for their dinner. The children have been collected by their parents, the house has been tidied and the goopins have been locked up for the night. The sun is setting and, beyond the kitchen window, the sky glows red and orange. "There is nothing on this earth that could persuade me to return to Blackmoon Coven," she tells Polly firmly. "Especially after hearing how much worse it has become."

Buster shrugs and widens his eyes at Polly. He can feel how desperate she is and he **shrinks in empathy**.

"But Aunt Hilda!" Polly begs again, her throat tight. "We *need* you. Witches are afraid that monsters are going to attack our town. Some of them are even saying there's going to be a war! We need you to come back and stop it. The stones say Blackmoon Coven needs a Silver Witch to fix this mess and I can't do it. I'm just a kid!" She pulls the little pouch out of her pocket and tips the stones onto the table.

"*You're* that Silver Witch, Aunt Hilda. These were meant for *you*," she insists.

"Polly, I don't think you understand," Aunt Hilda says, wiping her hands on her apron. She pulls up a chair to sit at the table and takes both of Polly's hands in hers. "Even if I *wanted* to come back to Blackmoon Coven, which I don't, there is absolutely nothing I can do. I may have been born a Silver Witch, but I haven't practiced magic since I left home at sixteen."

"But you showed me some magic just now!" Polly pleads. "Please, Aunt Hilda. You could do magic again if you wanted to. It doesn't just go away!"

"Oh, Polly. That wasn't *magic*. Those were

just some fancy tricks I learned from my days at Miss Madden's. Any old witch can turn tea into snails."

"Really?" says Buster, looking at Polly with interest.

"True magic is a force, not a gimmick," says Aunt Hilda, frowning. "True magic takes *years* to cultivate. And anyway, I'm not interested." She heads back over to the stove. "Blackmoon Coven is dead to me now. It's a nasty place and it deserves everything it has coming to it," she snaps. "It doesn't even deserve *you*, Polly. You are much too good for a horrible town like that." She turns back to look at Polly and Buster. "Come and live with me," she says, smiling again. "Both of you! You'd be much happier here. And the kids would love you!"

Polly's mouth drops open in disbelief. Of course there is nothing she would like more than to run away from all the danger that is going on back home and just live here with her aunt in the peaceful valley, but the fact that her aunt would suggest this fills her with rage. Her heart begins to pound and red swirls appear in the sides of her vision. She feels her cheeks get hot.

"Are you *really* telling me just to give up on Blackmoon Coven?" she seethes. "That's my *home* you're talking about! That's where all my *family* is. And yours, too, in case you'd forgotten? Just because you ran away doesn't mean there aren't witches there who still care about you. Did you really think it didn't hurt my mother's feelings when you didn't come back for my dad's funeral? You're our *family*, Aunt Hilda! Our *only* family!"

Polly's head begins to **fizz**. All around her, things in the kitchen begin to **quiver** and **spark**. A cup lifts into the air and hovers above the tablecloth. The lamp dims and brightens, and a spoon rattles in the sink. Polly closes her eyes and takes some deep, slow breaths to try to calm down.

She hears Buster's worried voice beside her. "Polly?" he whispers nervously. She feels his gentle paw on her arm.

Polly counts to three in her head. Then she opens her eyes and narrows them on her aunt, who is surveying the room in alarm. Polly's voice comes out low and bitter. "Do you know what?" she growls. "If you really don't care even one little bit about the place you were born and the family you left behind then you are even worse than my mother says. You aren't wild and wayward at all! You aren't even an adventurer. You're just a *coward*."

Buster gasps.

Aunt Hilda's face grows pale and Polly instantly regrets what she has said. She drops her head in shame and all the racketing objects in the room grow still. "I'm sorry," she mumbles, and tears spill down her cheeks. "I'm just so tired of all this. I wish it would all go away. I wish everything would go back to how it was before those silly miners woke that silly gorvan!"

Aunt Hilda sits beside Polly and brushes away her tears. "I'm sorry, Polly. Maybe you're right. Maybe I *am* a coward."

"Oh, I wouldn't say that!" Buster interrupts, trying to be kind, but Aunt Hilda only smiles at him, then turns back to Polly.

"Maybe you thought I was brave and adventurous because I've traveled the globe, but the truth is I'm not half as brave as you, Polly," she continues. "Unlike you, I couldn't face the world I was born into, so I ran away. I'm not proud of that. But I am trying to make up for it now. I have a good life here and the villagers count on me, as do all those children you met today. This is where I can make a difference. I'm teaching all those children to read and write. There isn't anyone else here who can do that for them. I know it may only be a small difference. I know it may not seem a very impressive thing for a Silver Witch to be doing. But if I can bring up all the children in this village to treat each other with kindness and fairness, then this makes me happy. *This* is my calling now, Polly. This is something I can do for the world."

Polly breathes in deeply and rests her chin in her hands. She feels more tired than she has ever been. It has been such a long and exhausting day, and the thought of returning to Blackmoon Coven without Aunt Hilda sucks the last little bit of energy out of her. Buster moves his chair closer to Polly so that she can feel him by her side. His **warmth** comforts her a little.

"I know it might be hard for you to believe, but the stones chose *you*," Aunt Hilda continues gently. "And now I see why. You are a powerful witch, Polly. More powerful than I could have ever hoped to be. You just don't know how to control that power yet." She tips Polly's face up to look her in the eye. "Your magic is getting stronger, isn't it?" she says, her voice low and serious.

Polly nods. She feels a familiar flutter of fear and excitement when she thinks about this, and wipes a tear from her cheek with the back of her hand.

"It sure is!" Buster offers. "You should have seen what Polly did to the kids at her school!" He giggles. "I'll give you a clue: they'll be hopping mad at Polly now!" He elbows Polly, grinning goofily. "Hopping mad. Get it? *Hopping* mad."

Polly thinks she glimpses the tiniest bit of fear in her aunt's eyes before it disappears again. "That's what I thought," Aunt Hilda says, ignoring Buster, who is still laughing at his own joke. "I bet you used to feel ill after doing a big spell, but now you don't?"

"Yes," says Polly. "How did you know?"

Aunt Hilda sighs. "That happened to me, too. It's a sign that your powers are growing.

I'll bet the spells are coming out of you more often now, too, aren't they? And much more easily?"

Polly nods.

Aunt Hilda pauses. "I know you might not think much of me now, but can I just give you some advice?"

Polly nods again.

"Every time you do a spell from now on, your magic will become stronger and stronger," Aunt Hilda says. "It is the gift given to you when you are born a Silver Witch. But the time has come to decide what *kind* of Silver Witch you will become. Every time you do magic from a place of fear or anger, it will take you in one direction.

And the further you go along in this direction, the harder it will be for you to return."

She takes a deep breath. "From all you told me about Deidre Halloway, I can see that she creates magic from fear and hate — and look at what she has become. Yes, she may be a powerful Black Witch, but what use is power when it is only used to hurt others? You, Polly, as a Silver Witch, can also choose to find power in love and kindness." She rests a hand on Polly's arm. "But it won't be easy. In fact, it may be the hardest choice of all. I knew I didn't have that kind of strength and courage, so it was easier for me just to give up magic completely. I'm sorry this responsibility was passed down to you. It can be a heavy load to bear. And I'm so sorry I'm not the aunt you were hoping I would be."

Polly breathes in deeply. She picks up the three small stones and they *glow gently* in her hand. Deep down, somehow, she has always known this is what her aunt would say. The stones told her it would take a Silver Witch to stop the war in Blackmoon Coven. And deep down, she knew that Silver Witch was her. She just didn't want to hear it. "That's OK," she says quietly. "I guess I always knew it would be up to me. I was just *really* hoping I was wrong."

Aunt Hilda wraps her arms around Polly and the jumble of feelings inside her melt away.

Anger, fear, despair. She leans into her aunt and feels her solid warmth, and they stay quiet like that for a long moment. Polly knows the person who has brought them together is her father, and she feels a pang of longing for him. It never seems to go away.

Fourteen

After dinner, Polly, Buster and Aunt Hilda each take a mug of warm goopin milk and honey out to the wicker sofa on the porch. Polly sinks into the soft cushions and gazes up at the sky. Her eyelids are heavy and she feels the warmth of Buster on one side of her and her aunt on the other.

The stones are hot in her pocket and she knows they probably have something important to tell her. All kinds of crazy things are probably happening in Blackmoon Coven. But just for a moment she would like to rest. Just for one small moment, she would like to do nothing except listen to the gentle bleating of the goopins in the darkness, with her best friend by her side. So she puts the pouch on the floor beside her and together they watch the stars sparkle like jewels scattered across the black velvet sky.

"Ooh look," Buster murmurs, just as Polly's eyelids are beginning to close. "Can you see that weird light in the distance?"

Polly leans her head against him and listens to his voice gently rumble deep in his chest. She loves his familiar smell of moss and jamcakes.

The wicker sofa creaks as her aunt leans forward to peer up at the sky. "What light?" Aunt Hilda asks Buster.

"Over there," Buster says. He shifts his arm out from under Polly's head to point up into the sky.

"Buster! I was nearly asleep," Polly grumbles.

"Um … Polly?" Buster's voice sounds a little more urgent. He shakes her gently. "I think you should take a look. I think we may have seen that light somewhere before. It kind of … it kind of looks like a *mist* actually. A *purple* mist."

Polly's eyes snap open. Her heart jumps about in her chest. She stares up into the sky, up where Buster is pointing. "No," she says quietly. "It can't be. No, no, no. That's impossible!"

She reaches for the stones. They are glowing so hot now, she can barely pick them up. Polly scolds herself for putting them down. For letting herself believe she could relax for a moment.

As soon as they are in her palm they send an image into her mind. Polly grabs Buster's paw and jerks him upright beside her. "Oh no, oh no, oh no. Buster, we have to go! We have to go now!" She jumps up and shoves the little bag of stones deep in her pocket.

Buster has shrunk to Polly's size and turned gray with **worry**.

"What is it? What is it, Polly?" Aunt Hilda implores as she follows them to where the broomstick is propped against the house. "Do you really have to leave now? It's late! Polly!"

The purple mist is now almost thick enough to blot out the stars. Polly knows there is only one thing that can create a mist like that. One thing that can block out the stars and all hope for their future. And while Polly has been snoozing on her aunt's porch, sipping goopin milk and dreaming of quieter days, that one thing is now heading straight for Blackmoon Coven.

She swings a leg over the broomstick handle. Buster jumps on behind her without a single complaint and wraps his arms tightly around her waist. She can feel his solid, loyal heart beating right through his chest. She twists the end of the handle until the **FLY** light turns green, then turns to face her Aunt Hilda one last time.

Her aunt's eyes are alight with worry. "Polly, please! Tell me! What's going on? Where are you going? Can't this wait until tomorrow?"

Polly sucks in some cool night air and tries to steady her voice. She looks straight into her aunt's eyes. "I know you don't want anything to do with Blackmoon Coven," she says, "but everyone I've ever loved lives in that town and I need to warn them of what's coming. I have no idea how it got out of the mines, but this is worse than just a war between witches and monsters, Aunt Hilda. Much, much worse."

She lifts the broomstick into the air and hovers above her fretting aunt.

"But what's coming, Polly?" Aunt Hilda pleads. "What did you see in that purple mist?"

"Aunt Hilda. You *know* what makes that purple mist. I told you today when I told you about the mines."

And as Polly flies straight up into the dark night sky, she glimpses the look of horror on her aunt's face as she finally understands.

"The gorvan!"

Polly sees the word form on her aunt's lips,
and even the shape of it chills her to the bone.

Fifteen

Polly flies faster than she ever has before, crouched low against the broomstick handle. Buster, curled up tight and small, hangs on for dear life behind her. The ground whirrs far beneath them and the purple mist laps at their heels. She feels its dampness soaking into her skin, and fights hard not to let it affect her.

She remembers being back in the mines, when the gorvan's mist made her hate Buster. Buster, her dearest, truest friend! Polly is determined not to let that happen again. She flies even faster so she can leave the damp badness behind.

The night air is **icy.** It burns her cheeks and water streams from her eyes, but Polly flies straight and true, following the guidance of the moon.

Suddenly Polly hears an **almighty crack,** like lightning, and Buster is thrown from the stick.

"Buster!" she screams. She swerves her broomstick around to find herself face-to-face with Deidre Halloway, wand held high.

"You!"

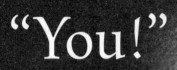

Polly gasps.
"What have

you done?"

"Did you really think I wouldn't come back for him?" Mrs. Halloway cackles. "That dirty, dangerous monster is the reason I was *banished* from Blackmoon Coven!"

"Buster!" Polly screams again, frantically searching the skies. And then she sees him. Caught below them in Mrs. Halloway's spell, but still dangling high above the ground. "What are you doing?" Polly cries. "Let him go! Let him go!"

"You want me to let him go?" Mrs. Halloway smiles, dropping Buster another three feet in the air.

"No, stop!" Polly yells. "Don't drop him!" The ground spins sickeningly below them.

Polly flies down to try to save Buster, but Mrs. Halloway has put a force field around him, and it's too strong for her to break through.

Buster's eyes are as wide as dinner plates and he has shrunk to the size of a bortal. "Don't be scared, Buster! I'll rescue you!" Polly tells him, but her fear is so loud in her head she can hardly hear herself think. She flies back to where Mrs. Halloway is still hovering, a nasty smile splitting open her pale face.

"What are you doing?" Polly cries. "What do you want?" Her heart is racing so fast that she can't breathe properly. She tries to summon a spell, but Mrs. Halloway notices, and a green bolt shoots out from the tip of her wand and fastens Polly's hands to her stick.

"It's a good one, isn't it?" she says, admiring her gleaming new wand.

As they hover there, the purple mist grows around them until it is almost as thick and cold as fog.

"But of course, as you would know, an ordinary witch's magic couldn't do anything as powerful as this without a little help." Mrs. Halloway smiles, and as Polly watches, she dips her long-nailed fingers into her cape and pulls out a small pouch of stones, almost identical to hers.

Polly gasps.

"You didn't think you were the only one to be given stones from the mines, did you?" Mrs. Halloway chuckles. "My brother was in those mines too, remember?"

Polly does remember Mrs. Halloway's brother. She met his ghost in the mines. She pictures his face, full of regret and sorrow. She tries to remember what he told her about Mrs. Halloway, but her mind is **muddled with fear**. If only she had Miss Spinnaker's velvet bag of letters with her. She glances down to see Buster hanging far beneath them and her heart pounds loudly in her ears. She tries to lift her hands from the broomstick, but they're stuck fast.

"Every time you activate *your* stones I hear you through *my* stones. I know everywhere you've been and everything you've done. And that silly Mayor of yours thought she could just banish me from Blackmoon Coven." She throws her head back and laughs loudly like it's the most ridiculous thing she's ever heard.

"Banish *me*? What was she thinking? She has no say over me! I am now the most powerful witch in Blackmoon Coven! I have magic stones powerful enough to wake a gorvan!" she says, swinging her hands out toward the roiling purple fog.

"No!" Polly gasps, her hands clammy on the broomstick and her eyes stinging with the purple mist. "Why would you *do* such a thing? You can't let the gorvan out! It will destroy Blackmoon Coven!"

"Blackmoon Coven is already destroyed," Mrs. Halloway sneers. "My home was once a powerful witches' town, full of magic and sorcery, and now it is a place crawling with dangerous monsters. You know this, Polly. Don't pretend you don't. You saw those monsters building an army in the forest. You know they are planning to take over Blackmoon Coven."

She tosses her head back again and cackles, bobbing in the cool night air beside Polly. Then she turns back to Polly and sneers nastily. "But you, you meddling little piece of moledust, turned the whole town against me, didn't you? Even my own daughter! But don't you worry, Polly Proggett. With the gorvan beside me, nothing will be able to stop us. The gorvan and I will chase the monsters from this town once and for all!"

Polly feels the stones in her pocket, so hot now they almost burn her skin. She peers into the choking mist and her skin crawls in fear. Then a memory flits around her mind like a butterfly. *Papa said if I keep these stones safe, no one will be able to wake the gorvan again!*

But Mrs. Halloway seems to know this, too. She smiles. "The stones my brother gave me were enough to wake the gorvan. But of course, after I reached it, deep underground, what did I discover?

Six stones were taken from the gorvan's cave, not three. And who should have the other three stones I need to make it do my bidding?" She holds her stones close to her ear, pretending they are speaking to her. Then she claps her hand over her mouth and opens her eyes wide in fake surprise. "No! Really? You're telling me it's our dear Polly Proggett? Well, I never!" She laughs at her joke, then looks down her nose to where Buster is still hanging in her spell, far below. "So, if you would like to rescue your beloved monster friend, the choice is easy, my dear. Hand me your stones and I will let him go."

"No!" Buster yells from far below. "Don't do it, Polly!"

Mrs. Halloway cackles, waves her wand and drops him another three feet closer to the ground.

Polly screams. "Unlock my hands and I'll give them to you!" she yells, trying to pull herself free from the broomstick handle again.

Mrs. Halloway sneers. "As if I'd fall for *that* old trick!" she says, flying in close. She points her wand at Polly, who feels just one of her hands release from the broomstick.

"Polly!" Buster yelps from far below. "Don't give them to her. Please keep my family safe!"

Mrs. Halloway sighs and rolls her eyes, like she's terribly bored of the whole conversation, and points her wand in Buster's direction.

"No!"

Polly screams. She can't let Buster fall any farther! Quickly, she darts her free hand into her pocket and tosses the pouch of stones into the air as high and as far as she can. It's all she can think of doing to save him.

Mrs. Halloway spins her broomstick around to catch them, but not before she has sent another spark shooting from her wand.

Polly looks down
just in time to see
Buster tumble
through the
night
sky.

Sixteen

Polly zooms down to the cold, dark earth, to where Buster has fallen, her heart thumping madly. He's sprawled on the ground, and his big, rumbly, chuckly body is weirdly quiet.

"Buster! Wake up!" she says desperately, shaking him gently. "Are you OK?"

She can see that he is still breathing, but even

when she shakes him harder, his eyes remain shut.

"I hate you, Deidre Halloway!" she shouts up into the night sky, but Mrs. Halloway has long gone and Polly's words fall back to the ground like rain.

"Buster, please!" she sobs. "Please wake up! You're my bestest friend in this whole universe! There is nothing or no one in the world I love as much as you!"

Polly thinks back to all the spells she has learned at school, but not a single one of them has prepared her for something like this. She wishes she had the magic stones. They would tell her what to do.

Just as she is thinking this, a strange
sensation tingles in the center of her palm.
It becomes warmer and warmer until
soon her whole hand has begun to burn.
And as it burns, it sends warmth
along her freezing arms and legs and
into her aching chest until finally
a clear pink light fills her mind.

Polly sits up. She wipes her eyes and
looks at her palm, where the burning
feeling is coming from. There, to her complete
astonishment, are three round marks in the
shape of the magic stones. And as she stares
down at the marks, suddenly she knows
exactly what she has to do.

Polly places both her hands on Buster's quiet chest, just above his gently beating heart. Then she summons up all her love for him. She pictures every moment they have spent together: sees them in their tree, in the forest, in the mines. She sees Buster at her window. She pictures his good, kind face, always there for her, always ready to make her laugh when she is feeling bad. And despite the heavy sadness in her chest, a smile stretches across her face.

"I won't let you down, Buster," she whispers, and closes her eyes.

Polly draws a spell up into her body like she has so many times before. But this one feels different. This one is cool and blue and it seeps through her body like water. She breathes deeply, calmly, and then she **fills her heart with love**. It roars out of her chest and along her arms like a clean ocean wave. When she opens her eyes again, her mind is calm and clear and she feels no sickness at all.

She knows the spell has worked.

The first sound she hears is Buster's tummy rumbling with hunger.

It is the best sound she has ever heard.

Seventeen

Polly takes Buster straight home. They hardly talk at all except to say how grateful they are to have each other. Buster is exhausted and achy and she knows he needs to sleep for her healing spell to make him completely better. She carries him carefully on the broomstick in front of her, arms wrapped around him, and lands on his windowsill in the dead of night. His window is unlocked and she manages to help him crawl through, and tucks him into his bed.

Then she creeps quietly back to her house to collect the blue velvet bag she has stashed at the bottom of her cupboard. Deep within are the letters from the lost loved ones whose ghosts once haunted the Hollow Valley Mines. She suspects she might need them to prove whose side she is on. Now that she knows it's up to her to save Blackmoon Coven, she'll need all the help she can get.

As she passes her mother's room, Polly hovers in the doorway, just for a moment, to gaze at her mother's sleeping face, and the worry lines etched into her forehead. *It will all be over soon,*

Mama. I promise, she whispers. *I'm so sorry I'm not the witch you wanted me to be. But I think I am learning to be the witch I am.*

The next morning, Polly wakes up on Buster's floor, Miss Spinnaker's blue velvet bag under her head as a pillow. She can hear Buster calling her gently and sits up stiffly, stretching out her aching limbs.

Buster limps over to the window. "Polly," he says. "Come and see!"

Polly stumbles over to stand beside him. She hears them before she sees them. Crowds of angry monsters marching down their street.

Monsters she knows from all around their town. There is the old monster from the marketplace. There is the monster who cleans their school. There is the monster who Polly sees every day on the bus and always smiles at her, but who she has never spoken to.

Dozens of monsters have taken the day off work to march for their rights. Monsters who have had enough of being treated badly by witches. They carry placards and posters and are heading toward the Town Hall.

"Equal rights for monsters!" they chant. "Equal rights for monsters!"

They look **angry** and **determined**.

Polly remembers what Milly told her. Anger can start a war, but also a revolution. This is the revolution these once peaceful monsters are calling for. They have had enough of being treated unfairly by witches. And Polly completely understands. But the clouds above them are tinged with purple and Polly knows the monsters have no idea of the danger they are in.

"I have to warn them!" Polly cries. "The gorvan is on its way!"

"I'll come with you!" says Buster, but Polly can see him wince in pain and she knows he needs to rest.

"No, please stay here and let our moms know we are safe," she insists. "They'll be worried about us! Besides," she says, pulling the velvet bag over her shoulder and grabbing the broomstick, "I'll be quicker without you." She grins at him to show she is not afraid, but secretly her belly is **full of butterflies.**

Buster pretends to look disappointed, but Polly can see he is relieved he doesn't have to get on a broomstick again.

Polly opens the window and climbs up onto the sill, broomstick between her knees. Then she turns the handle to switch it on and **soars into the sky,** over the monsters filling the street. She has to stop them before it is too late.

"Stop! Go home!" Polly yells down to the monsters. "You are all in danger! The gorvan is coming!"

But their angry chanting makes it impossible for her to be heard. They have been too angry for too long and nothing will stop them now. Especially not a small witch hovering above them on a broomstick.

As Polly follows them toward town, she sees monsters raging up and down the streets, swinging from street signs and throwing rocks at windows. These are just angry monsters from the town, not even the Amber Skull Forest Gang, but already the destruction they have caused is terrible.

When Polly finally reaches the town square, she sees it is already crowded with monsters. Smoke rises from a huge bonfire. In the distance, Polly sees what she has been dreading. A black haze of witches on broomsticks approaches. Polly recognizes their purple sashes and the flash of silver lining from the long black capes that whip around them. This is the Central Patrol. Polly's stomach seizes in fear. Monsters may be fearless and strong, but the Mayor's law enforcers have magic on their side. The monsters don't stand a chance.

Sure enough, Polly sees the first witch pull a wand from her cape and aim at a monster below. A *silver current* shoots from the tip and strikes the monster square in the forehead. He is flung backward across the cobblestones and pinned to the ground. His great hairy arms and legs shake and quiver with magic. One by one, the witches pull wands from their capes and shoot down the monsters; big, small, young, old.

Polly's eyes fill with tears as she watches the chaos unfold beneath her. *This is everything that Mrs. Halloway wanted,* she thinks angrily. *Look what her hatred has created! Witches and monsters turning against each other.*

Some of the bigger monsters **roar** and **leap** from buildings to try to catch the witches zooming among them, but they are defenseless against magic. One by one, they are pinned to the ground and are left trapped, frozen, eyes goggling. Even the weaker, smaller monsters who try to escape are caught by the Central Patrol and flung to the ground.

Polly flies around the town square, careful to avoid the Central Patrol. She has to make them understand the danger they are in, but while monsters and witches are fighting each other, she knows there is no way they will listen to her.

Suddenly her palm begins to tingle and an idea pops into her head. *The Mayor!* she thinks. *I have to tell Mayor Redwolf the gorvan is coming. If she can stop the Central Patrol fighting the monsters, maybe she can make them fight the gorvan instead!*

She lands her broomstick near the Town Hall and is just about to step off when she feels a strong claw grab her from behind. She spins around and comes face-to-face with an enormous monster. He is green and scaly, with a long wide tail and sharp tusks sticking out of his face. But before Polly can even raise her arms to do a spell, the monster tosses her over his great muscled shoulder and bounds toward the Town Hall. He pulls open the heavy wooden door and leaps into the foyer, just as a bolt of silver magic strikes the ground behind them.

Eighteen

"I got one!" the monster roars. "I got one!" He carries Polly above his head in triumph and gallops toward the large wooden door of the grand meeting room, plonking Polly down onto the floor in front of him. Polly picks herself up and dusts herself off, then checks that none of her precious letters have fallen out of the blue velvet bag at her hip.

"Excuse me! Do you *mind*?" she says, trying to sound braver than she feels. "Don't you know who I am? I'm Polly Proggett. I'm a *friend* of monsters!"

The big green monster blinks at her.

"Polly!" comes a familiar voice, and Polly looks up to see Domsley, the big ginger monster from the Amber Skull Forest Gang. He is standing guard in front of the door to the meeting room. Zeke, the not-so-friendly guard, stands on the other side.

"Oh, slimy snakebile!" Zeke snarls, rolling his eyes. "Not you again. Who coulda guessed if there's trouble you'd be around? Tie 'er up and throw 'er in the cells with all the other traitors!" he commands. "She's the worst of the lot."

"Wait!" says Polly. "Zeke! Domsley! You have to listen to me. We're all in danger. The gorvan is coming! Mrs. Halloway let it out of the mines and they are heading straight for Blackmoon Coven. We have to tell the Mayor!"

"Ha!" Zeke says, rolling his mean little eyes again. "She just says any old lie, this one. Pugsler! I said tie 'er up. That's an order!"

The green monster grabs her arm, but Polly pulls away.

"Domsley?" Polly pleads. "You believe me, don't you? You must remember me and my friend Buster. I'm on your side, remember? My *best friend* is a monster!"

Domsley chews his lip and rocks from side to side, his brow furrowing, unable to meet Polly's gaze.

"Well, where is he then?" Zeke snarls. "Why ain't he here with you now if you're such good friends, eh? I don't believe a thing you say, you little wormy. You're all traitors, you witches. Every last one of you. Even that teacher of yours who tried to make our leader, Carmen, talk to your Mayor. Fat lotta good that's done us now, innit?" He gestures at the window to the flashes of magic from the Central Patrol.

Polly looks out and sees the small square of gray sky gradually turning purple. **"Please! Zeke! Domsley! Look outside!** That's the purple mist of the gorvan. It's on its way. If we don't do something, it will destroy our whole town!"

Domsley gasps and claps his big paw over his mouth, his eyes wide.

Zeke frowns at the purpling sky and pulls at his lip nervously. Polly knows all monsters believe in gorvans. Monsters believe in all the spirits of the land and sea and sky. It is only witches who don't believe there could be a power greater than theirs. But she can see Zeke still doesn't want to trust her.

"Look! I've been in the Hollow Valley Mines and seen the gorvan's mist!" She dips her hand into the blue velvet bag and pulls out a handful of letters. "Here! I have proof." She flicks through the letters until she finds the one she's after. "Your dad worked with my dad in the mines, didn't he? I met their ghosts when Buster and I were hiding in there from Mrs. Halloway. Look! I have a letter from his ghost for you!"

Polly thrusts the scrap of paper into Zeke's hands and watches his face as he reads it. She sees his eyes skim the lines twice, then a third time, his face **slowly crumpling** as the words sink in. Words that could have come

from no one but his father. He looks at Polly,
his eyes wide and glistening.

"This is from my da?" he croaks.

Polly nods somberly.

"You saw 'is ghost?"

Polly nods again. "He stayed behind with the ghosts of all the other miners to protect us from the gorvan. But now Mrs. Halloway has set it free, and it's not far away! We have to hurry!"

Zeke looks back out the window, wiping his tears with the back of his claw. "But … but this is terrible!" he gasps. "The gorvan will destroy our whole town!"

"That's what I've been trying to tell you!" Polly says desperately. "We have to stop it. We need to tell Mayor Redwolf! She may be able to get the Central Patrol to fight off the gorvan before it reaches us." She pushes past the monsters toward the door to the main meeting room.

"Um … you won't find her in there," Domsley mumbles, his voice almost apologetic. He winces as he holds up a big brass key ring with three long keys dangling from it.

"Are you serious?" Polly gasps. "You kidnapped the *Mayor*?"

"Those were our orders!" Zeke snaps. But he grabs the keys from Domsley and scuttles down the corridor toward the prison cells.

Domsley winks at Polly as they jog along behind him.

Nineteen

"You!" Zeke commands, unlocking the door to the cell and pulling Mayor Redwolf out. "You can go free! The rest of you will stay here for ransom."

He locks the cell again, and Polly gasps when she sees who else is in there.

"Miss Spinnaker!" Polly cries. "Flora! Mortimer!"

Miss Spinnaker rushes to the bars of the cell. "Please!" she begs Zeke. "My mother is old and frail. Leave me in here if you like, but let her go!"

"Our orders were to lock up as many witches as we can! And monster traitors!" Zeke says firmly, glaring at Miss Spinnaker's monster stepfather, Mortimer.

"This is not right!" Mayor Redwolf says, her face steely with anger. "There is no excuse for locking up children or the elderly. I am certain Carmen would never stand for it!"

"Excuse me!" Flora calls out indignantly. "I'm not *that* old, thank you very much!"

"Zeke," Domsley mutters. "We can't leave them here. Not with the gorvan on its way!"

"The gorvan?" Miss Spinnaker says, glaring at Polly. "What in blinking bats is he talking about?"

Polly feels her cheeks redden. "It's a long story, Miss Spinnaker, and I haven't been exactly truthful with you. I'm sorry. But all you need to know for now is that Mrs. Halloway has woken the gorvan that lives in the Hollow Valley Mines. And they are heading straight for Blackmoon Coven," Polly tells her. "She thinks she can control it with the magic stones. But she has no idea what she has really done! The gorvan will get bigger and stronger when it sees all the fighting going on outside because it feeds off anger and hate. Soon it will get so strong even Mrs. Halloway won't be able to control it. We have to hurry!"

Miss Spinnaker frowns in disbelief. But then they feel it. A sudden drop in temperature and the air becomes damp and hard to breathe. Polly claps her hand over her mouth as she recognizes the **dank sour smell** seeping into the building.

"Oh no!" she cries. "We're too late! It's already here!"

"But that's impossible," Miss Spinnaker stammers. "There's no such thing as gorvans!"

"Of course there is!" Mortimer says, his face buckling in fear. "What else could make a mist like this?"

"Don't breathe it in!" Polly warns. "It will make you turn against each other. Think good thoughts and you can keep it out of you. Mayor Redwolf, you have to call off the Central Patrol. They are fighting the monsters out there when they should be fighting the gorvan!"

"Leave it to me!" Mayor Redwolf says. "But you'll need to return our wands," she insists, glaring at Zeke. He hesitates, then reaches for the bag on Domsley's back to pull out two wands. The Mayor and Miss Spinnaker each hold up their right hands and their wands fly into their open palms, just as the temperature drops again. Polly begins to shiver.

"Come on!" Mayor Redwolf shouts, leading the way. All of them follow her, Mortimer carrying Flora on his big, broad shoulders. The air has become putrid and their eyes sting with the purple mist. Polly coughs as it fills her lungs, but she keeps focusing on Buster, the kindest monster she knows, to keep her mind clear.

They run past the grand meeting room just as its enormous wooden doors swing open. The gang of rebel monsters from the Amber Skull Forest tumble out, **coughing** and **spluttering,** including Carmen, their leader, who spots their prisoners escaping. She blinks in disbelief as she sees that her guards are not running *after* their prisoners, but *with* them! "What in dark moons is going on?" she yells.

"The gorvan is here! The gorvan is here!" Domsley yells back.

They burst out of the Town Hall into the main square and look around them in horror. The air is thick with **poisonous purple fog**, and the witches and monsters are locked in a furious battle. More monsters have joined the fight. Some of them have managed to pull witches from their broomsticks, but most of them lie writhing and howling, held to the ground with magic, while the Central Patrol spin above them, shooting sparks from their wands.

Mayor Redwolf strides out into the middle of the square and stares into the sky, her eyes flaming. She holds her wand high.

"Stop!"

she roars at the witches flying overhead, and her powerful voice fills the square. "Stop! Now!" she commands. "Central Patrol. Listen to me!"

The patrol circle above her, their eyes shifting uncertainly, wands outstretched. Clouds of purple mist billow around them, seeping into their lungs and skin.

The town square grows suddenly quiet.

Then they all hear it. A long, low **screech,** like **nails along metal,** and Polly looks up in horror to where the sound has come from.

There is nasty Deidre Halloway, bobbing about in the sky, **cackling madly.** She aims her wand and a dark black hole opens up in the huge swirling purple cloud that has gathered above them. A **big blob of slime** drops down through the fog onto the clock tower below.

Mrs. Halloway shrieks with laughter. "You think you can banish *me* from Blackmoon Coven?" she screeches over the noise. "Look at me now! I have the *gorvan* on my side!"

Polly looks up at Mayor Redwolf through the swirling fog.

"Well …?" the Mayor says to Polly in her deep and serious voice.

In a terrifying moment of clarity, Polly understands that the Mayor is looking to her to know what to do next. She realizes she is the only witch in Blackmoon Coven who has ever had any experience of gorvans and so, in a way, that makes *her* the expert! This thought would be funny if it weren't so scary. She clears her throat, her heart racing, and suddenly wishes all the witches in her spells class could see her now.

As they watch,
trembling in fear,
a long purple tentacle
unfurls from the black
hole Deidre has made,
followed by another
and another.

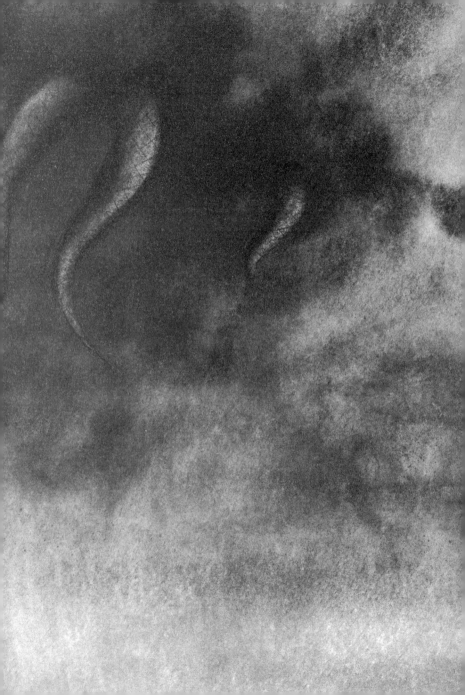

"Um ... tell them not to breathe its mist in," Polly shouts to the Mayor, her legs shaking. "Tell them to think about something good, or to picture someone they love. Tell them not to be scared. The gorvan will only get bigger and stronger if they are angry or afraid."

Mayor Redwolf's voice rings loud and clear above the chaos as she relays Polly's instructions. The witches circle nervously, edging away from the clock tower and the big black gash in the purple cloud.

Even if they have never believed in such a thing before, at that moment every one of them, witch, warlock or monster, knows the stuff of their most frightening childhood nightmares has come true.

"Patrol!" the Mayor shouts even louder. "Aim your wands!"

The circling black flock of witches point their wands toward the thick purple cloud where the gorvan's tentacles are **unfurling**, and look expectantly at the Mayor.

"All of you," the Mayor commands, "fire your wands ... Now!"

Bolts of silver shoot out of all of the wands at the same time, sending a **blinding flash of light** toward the purple cloud in the sky. The gorvan curls its tentacles back up into the safety of the cloud and the witches continue to shoot bolts from their wands to hold it there.

"Central Patrol, hold your magic strong!" Mayor Redwolf commands. Then she looks at Polly again.

Polly dips her hands into her pocket, but remembers the stones are no longer there. Deidre Halloway, circling high above the dark cloud of the gorvan, has all six of them. And she is using them to control the nightmare that is destroying their town.

Then suddenly Polly has the answer. The gorvan is powerless against kindness. She may not have the stones, but Polly knows in her heart what the witches and monsters of Blackmoon Coven have to do.

"They need to work together!"

she shouts to Mayor Redwolf. "If monsters and witches work together, it will shrink the gorvan. Trust me!"

The Mayor hesitates, but then, to Polly's surprise, Carmen steps up beside them and calls out at the top of her deep, loud voice. **"Monsters! Do whatever you can to help. We must stand beside the witches to protect our town!"**

Carmen picks up an enormous boulder and tosses it up into the sky with all her strength. It disappears into the giant purple cloud and Polly hears the gorvan screech and squeal as the rock lodges in its body. A thin hiss of gray mist **oozes** from the clouds.

The Amber Skull Forest Gang quickly moves into action. As the witches hold the gorvan back with the force of their magic, the monsters scrabble about for anything they can find to toss into the sky to scare away the gorvan.

The creature screeches and hisses,

and Polly is thrilled to see its purple cloud shredding in places and its tentacles shrinking. "It's working!" she shouts. "It's working!"

While the witches and monsters fight the gorvan, Miss Spinnaker dashes about the square with her wand, unlocking the frozen monsters from the cobblestones and setting them to work alongside the witches. Polly hesitates and then, glancing up at her teacher, she starts to do the same thing with a magic that is coming more and more naturally to her.

"Well, look at you!" Miss Spinnaker says, sounding impressed. "You can't mix a potion, but you can create magic from your fingertips. It looks like those stones really *did* know who they were choosing!"

Polly smiles proudly. "So, I won't be expelled from school, then?" she asks nervously.

Miss Spinnaker laughs. "Polly, why would Miss Madden's want to expel their most powerful witch? I can't guarantee that you won't end up with a whole lot of cleanup duty, though!"

Polly grins. She watches the witches and monsters fighting the gorvan side by side and feels more hopeful than she has in a long time. Even though burning globs of slime still **boil** and **spit** from the purple cloud, the noise of the gorvan is definitely becoming fainter.

This is the true heart of Blackmoon Coven, she thinks. *This is where the good is! When monsters and witches work together there is no way the gorvan can defeat them!*

But as Polly looks up at the sky, she spots something that makes her chest fill with anger. Mrs. Halloway circles high above them, flashing her wand at the gorvan's cloud, and each time she does, Polly sees it grow again.

Without a second thought, Polly grabs a nearby broomstick and climbs on.

"Wait, Polly! **Stop!**" Miss Spinnaker calls. "What are you doing?"

"I've got this!" Polly calls out over her shoulder. "Just trust me!"

Twenty

"Deidre Halloway sees Polly coming and flies away from the gorvan and the chaos below, higher and higher into the foggy purple sky. "Come and get me, little witch," she taunts, cackling loudly. "If you dare!"

Polly feels a boiling rage rise up through her and every inch of her skin burns hot. Her fingertips crackle and spark, and her eyes flash red with hate. There is no one in the world she hates more than this witch. This witch who hurt Buster. This witch who is determined to ruin everything Polly has ever loved.

She crouches low on her broomstick and flies faster and faster, directly upward, until Mrs. Halloway is within clear view. Then, full of anger, she flings out her hands and sends a scorching orange bolt straight toward the cackling witch.

Mrs. Halloway points her wand at Polly and strikes the bolt away. Her eyes **gleam** with excitement and intrigue. "That's more like it! Finally acting like a *real* witch, Miss Proggett!" She points her wand in Polly's direction, but Polly manages to dodge the bolt just in time. "Real witches are powerful. They do spells and create magic. Real witches don't hang about with filthy *monsters!*" She strikes Polly with her wand again. This time, it catches the bristles of Polly's broomstick and they burst into flames.

Polly points her fingers at the fire and puts it out. The broomstick **sputters** and **wobbles,** but Polly knows better than to look down. Soon the bristles grow back, stronger than before. Polly keeps her eyes trained on Mrs. Halloway, whose eyes widen in surprise, impressed by Polly's new magic.

"I hate you, I hate you, I hate you!" Polly hisses, her cheeks burning hot.

"Good!" Mrs. Halloway chuckles. "It feels good, doesn't it, Polly? To hate? It makes you feel strong and powerful." Mrs. Halloway brings her broomstick in closer and coasts alongside Polly. "Just think how powerful you could be, Polly," she coaxes. "I see it in you. You could be the strongest witch in this town. Just let the gorvan's mist inside you. Go on! Let your hatred fill you, Polly. And become the witch you were meant to be."

Polly closes her eyes and, for a moment, lets herself breathe in the gorvan's mist. She can't help it. Her thoughts burn with revenge and its icy damp fills her lungs. Electricity crackles along her limbs. Her body feels stronger and more powerful than it ever has, and when Polly glances down at her skin, she can see it is tinged with purple. Just like Mrs. Halloway's.

Mrs. Halloway cackles. "Look at you, Polly! Look at the power in you. Let the gorvan's mist fill you and you can do anything. Come and fight with me, Polly, and we will rid Blackmoon Coven of those nasty monsters for good."

She brings her broomstick in even closer. "You are too powerful a witch to be mixing with that foul monster, Polly," she hisses. "What's his name? Bumper? Bouncer?"

Polly turns her broomstick to face Mrs. Halloway and narrows her eyes. Her skin is now seeping with purple mist, and she feels a **fiery bloom** inside her chest. She curls back her lip and sneers. "There is nothing in this world that would make me side with you, Mrs. Halloway," she hisses, and for a second, she sees a glimmer of fear flit across her enemy's face. The sight makes her feel stronger than ever.

Polly closes her eyes and breathes the biggest, most ferocious magic into her body that she possibly can. Then she opens her eyes, flings out her hands and a blaze of fire roars from her fingertips, surrounding Mrs. Halloway in a huge ring of flames. The sky is lit in flickering red and Mrs. Halloway stares out of her fiery cage, eyes wide. Her mouth opens and closes, but Polly can't hear what she is saying above the roar of the flames and the rushing noise of the magic in her head. "His name is Buster, Mrs. Halloway," she says, calmly. "And he is my best friend."

All she needs to do is tighten the ring of flame and all of this will be over; Mrs. Halloway, the gorvan, and the hatred she has planted in this town.

All she needs to do is click her fingers and this evil witch will be no more.

But then Polly thinks of Malorie, Mrs. Halloway's daughter.

Malorie who teased Polly at school for being bad at spells, but who stood up for Polly and Buster in front of the mines. Malorie, who was able to be turned around by Buster's act of kindness. Polly knows what it is like to lose a parent. She knows that pain never goes away. She can't do that to Malorie.

She stares through
the flames and looks
into Mrs. Halloway's eyes.
She sees they are filled
with fear.

Polly realizes then that if she were to take Mrs. Halloway's life she would be no better than her worst enemy, and suddenly she understands what her aunt had been trying to tell her.

Every time you do a spell from now on, your magic will become stronger. It is the gift given to you when you were born a Silver Witch, but you have to decide what kind of Silver Witch you will become.

To destroy Mrs. Halloway would send Polly so far down the path of hatred she knows she could never return. This is the choice she gets to make as a Silver Witch.

Twenty-One

Polly closes her eyes and takes in a deep breath of the hot air around her. She pictures all the people she loves: her mother, her sister, her teacher, her aunt, and of course her dearest friend, Buster, who would be so sad if she did something so bad. Something so bad it would be impossible to come back from. She knows what kind of Silver Witch she wants to be. She has known it all along.

Polly breathes out and a long stream of hot, stinky, purple mist **oozes** from her nostrils and pours from her skin. She opens her eyes and sees it drift up and away from her, and **sizzle** in the burning flames. Polly lifts her hands and draws the ring of fire back into her fingertips. Mrs. Halloway bobs on her broomstick only a few feet away, her cheeks red and the tips of her hair singed.

"Ha! You didn't have the courage, did you?" she crows weakly. "You had the chance to vanquish your greatest enemy and here you are, still hesitating. What kind of witch *are* you, Polly?" she squawks.

Polly takes another deep breath and her

voice comes out calm and strong. "I'm a Silver Witch, Mrs. Halloway," she calls from a safe distance. "The most powerful witch of all. But not powerful in the way you want me to be. Powerful in the way *I* want to be."

Mrs. Halloway watches her carefully, waiting for another moment to strike.

"I feel sorry for you, Mrs. Halloway," Polly says. "I'm sorry you are so angry and afraid." And as Polly says it out loud, she begins to mean it. "How horrible to be so afraid of something that all you can think to do is destroy it. I know you are afraid of monsters," she goes on, swooping in and out of the fog. "That's why you hate them so much."

"Don't be silly, child!" Mrs. Halloway shrieks, shooting her wand at Polly again. "Me, afraid of monsters? What a ridiculous thing to say! Monsters are filthy, disgusting creatures and they are a danger to witches!"

Polly weaves in and out of the bolts from Mrs. Halloway's wand. In the distance, flashes from the Central Patrol's wands still strike the purple cloud and the gorvan shrieks and roars. Polly's voice grows stronger by the minute. "You know that's not true, Mrs. Halloway. You are just afraid of them. Your brother told me you have been scared of monsters your whole life," she shouts. "A monster gave you a fright once, when you were little, and since then you have always been afraid of them."

Mrs. Halloway's face twists up with anger. Purple steam **snorts** from her nostrils. "What do you know about my brother?" she hollers. "If he hadn't worked with those monsters he would still be alive today! And your father, too, Polly! Don't forget that! It's *monsters* who killed your father in those mines. Not the gorvan! It was the monsters who made that mine collapse and took my only brother!" she screams.

Polly ignores Mrs. Halloway's shrieking. She dips her hand into the velvet bag flapping at her waist. The letter she's seeking is easy to find because she's folded it into a small triangle. Of all the messages she has stored there, to be delivered to monsters and witches all over Blackmoon Coven, she knows this is the one that's needed most.

Mrs. Halloway watches Polly curiously as she unfolds the letter.

"Dear little sister," Polly reads aloud, glancing up at Mrs. Halloway to see her reaction.

Dear little sister, I am sorry to hear you have become so angry. Please don't be afraid of monsters. I loved working with these brave souls every day of my working life. Monsters are some of the best, most decent creatures I have ever had the fortune to know and it was an honor to work alongside them.
Signed,
Your brother, Bumkin.

"He told me you'd know it was him because no one ever called him that but you," Polly says.

She looks at Mrs. Halloway, whose face has drained of all color. "My brother!" she gasps, her voice choked up and squeaky. "Where did you see him? When did he tell you this?"

"In the mines," Polly says as she edges closer to Mrs. Halloway. She holds the note out toward her and it flutters in the wind. "I saw his ghost. And my father's, too."

Mrs. Halloway snatches the note and stares at it, her eyes wide. As she reads it, again and again, Polly brings her broomstick closer until she is bobbing alongside her in the swirling foggy air.

"We both lost family we loved in the mines, Mrs. Halloway," says Polly, quietly. "And so did many monsters."

Polly watches Mrs. Halloway's face crumple and her eyes flood with tears. She tips her head back and wails, clutching the little note to her chest. **"My brother! I miss him *so* much!"** she howls. "You have no idea how much it hurt when he died, Polly. I feel like a piece of me died, too."

"I know what that feels like, Mrs. Halloway," Polly says, her eyes pricking with tears. "And the pain doesn't go away. But you can make your heart grow **bigger** around it until the pain doesn't take up so much space."

Polly draws closer. She knows what she has to do. She just hopes it will work. Mrs. Halloway has been angry and afraid for so long now that Polly isn't sure she can help her. But she knows she has to try.

"If you can trust me I can maybe help you, Mrs. Halloway," she says gently. She holds out her hand. Mrs. Halloway flinches, but Polly keeps her hand outstretched.

"Please," Polly says gently. "Malorie needs you, Mrs. Halloway."

Mrs. Halloway looks at the note again. Then back at Polly. Her eyes are wide and frightened and full of tears, but slowly she holds out a trembling hand.

Polly takes Mrs. Halloway's
burning hand in hers.
She sees the trembling witch's skin
has turned a glistening sickly purple.

She closes her eyes. The cool blue spell she used on Buster **rolls up through her body.** She takes a deep breath and sends the spell straight through her fingertips and into Mrs. Halloway. As she does, a thick purple mist seeps out of Mrs. Halloway's skin and floats up into the sky. It disappears among the clouds. When Polly opens her eyes, Mrs. Halloway has become **wrinkled and pale,** like a balloon that has no air left in it, and her hair has turned completely white. Polly's spell has worked.

Polly understands at that moment that her aunt was right. Kindness is the most powerful spell of all.

Polly guides their broomsticks to the ground. When they land, Mrs. Halloway's whole body slumps. She folds the letter up tightly in her trembling fingers. "Thank you, Polly," she rasps. "My brother would be ashamed to see how angry I have become. I don't know why you saved my life, but all I can do is thank you."

Polly allows herself a small smile, but then quickly makes her face serious again. She holds out her hand. "You have something that belongs to me, Mrs. Halloway."

Mrs. Halloway rummages around in the folds of her long black cape for the two silk bags she has hidden there. She hesitates, then drops them into Polly's outstretched palm.

"Please take them back to the mines, Polly," she whispers, "and whatever you do, please make sure no one ever digs them up again. They have caused me nothing but trouble and pain."

Then she starts up her broomstick and flies off against the swirling purple sky, as far away from the danger as she can.

Polly tucks the six magic stones in her pocket and heads straight toward the mines.

Twenty-Two

*T*he mines are as horrible and desolate as they ever were, except this time, as Polly approaches, she sees that the purple haze has disappeared. She lands the broomstick and leans it against the entrance.

The last time she was here, she had Buster by her side. And her father's ghost was waiting below. This time, she is completely alone. But she is not afraid. Both her father and Mrs. Halloway's brother thought they were doing a good thing by taking the gorvan's stones from the mines to give to the witches they loved most in the world.

It's true that a gorvan's stones bring power to any witch who carries them, but too much power is never a good thing. Especially when it falls into the wrong hands. Polly pulls them out of her pocket and holds the two silk pouches in her left hand. She feels a little sad to be giving up the only thing her father passed down to her, but when she looks at her right palm she sees that the three pale circles still mark her skin.

You have taught me all I needed to know, and I

will always carry you with me, Polly smiles. *But I know now it's not these stones that showed me my true magic. It was your faith in me, Papa. I don't need them anymore. These stones can now go back to where they really belong.*

She steps into the mines and holds the pouches in front of her. They light up the long narrow tunnel, getting brighter and brighter as she travels deeper underground, until finally she reaches the chamber where she and Buster first met the ghosts.

Polly feels a sudden pang of longing for her father. She thinks of Mrs. Halloway and Zeke, and all the other witches and monsters who lost loved ones in these mines, and she knows she is not the only one who feels this deep, aching pain. And somehow, even though it doesn't make the pain go away, this thought makes her feel less alone. She takes a deep breath and walks into the chamber.

The gorvan's wall is gray and flat now that there is no mist seeping out. She approaches it nervously, running her hand across its rough surface to see if she can find a way in. Eventually, her fingers find a long, deep crevice. She pulls at it gently, but it won't budge.

Polly holds up the stones and they light up the crack. She closes her eyes. She only knows one gorvan spell, but she supposes it's worth a try.

*"Darkling day, drifting light
Keep you safe all through the night.
Sleep my child, your dreams are sound
While the gorvan's underground."*

She peers at the long crevice. At first nothing seems to happen. Then, to her surprise, the wall rolls back and inside is a glowing red cave, encrusted with crystals and gems.

Polly steps gingerly into the red cave. It is surprisingly warm in there and she notices the walls are moving slightly, almost like they are breathing.

Then she sees them. Six empty cavities where her father and Mrs. Halloway's brother had pried away the magic stones all those years ago. *Was that the beginning?* Polly wonders. *Was that one wrong act the start of this whole terrible story?*

Polly tips the colorful stones into her palm and examines them. Polly's stones are pink, amber and blue, but Mrs. Halloway's are emerald, white and purple. Purple as the gorvan's mist. Polly glances at all the stones embedded in the red wall. There are plenty of stones in blue and pink and amber, plenty in white and all the shades of green you could imagine, but there are no other stones in purple.

This must have been the most precious and

powerful stone of all, Polly realizes, as she holds it up to the glow of the sparkling wall. Deep within she sees a small red light, like a gorvan's eye, watching her, waiting to feed off her anger and fear. *No wonder it made Mrs. Halloway so unwell,* she thinks. *Lucky this wasn't a stone my father chose for me! Imagine how different all this could have been!*

Polly carefully places all the stones back into the empty cavities. She returns the purple one last and it sinks deep into the soft, sticky red surface with a hiss. She turns around to see what will happen next. She has no idea what to expect.

Then she hears it.

From far, far away. A **terrifying screeching** sound, becoming louder and louder. Soon the whole cave echoes with it. Polly squeezes her eyes shut and covers her ears with her hands.

Suddenly, the mine becomes deathly cold. She opens her eyes to see purple fog billowing into the chamber and her lungs and nostrils fill with its **rancid smell**. She runs out of the red cave, but it is too late.

Through the fog she sees the first tentacle creep around the corner of the chamber. Her heart pounds so fast she can barely breathe. She tries to run past, but another tentacle **whips** around the corner and wraps tightly around her waist. Polly feels herself being lifted up and she shuts her eyes tight. Her head **fizzes** with fear.

When she dares to open her eyes, she is staring straight into the glittering red eye of the gorvan. Its whole body fills the chamber, its tentacles pressed up against the curved walls. She feels the sting of their suckers through her clothing. Its lips **curl back** and it breathes cold **putrid air** into her face. Up close, it is more terrifying than she could have ever imagined. Polly tries to lift her arms to do a spell, but they are pinned to her sides by the gorvan's tight grip.

She has no idea how she is going to escape and

suddenly she realizes how silly she was to come alone. If only she had gone back to get Buster! What was she thinking, coming all this way without him? She may well be a Silver Witch, but even the most powerful witch couldn't possibly fight a gorvan on their own! *Buster! Help!* Polly thinks, hoping that somehow he might be able to hear her. *Buster, please! Come and save me!*

The gorvan's stomach rumbles loudly and Polly squeezes her eyes shut as it opens its huge **slimy** mouth.

But then Polly hears another noise. A strange noise that makes the gorvan blink and slide its eye to peer over her shoulder, its mouth still hanging open and dripping with drool. From far away, Polly hears the pounding of footsteps echoing throughout the mine. And the gasping of someone who is definitely out of breath.

"Wait!" comes a voice.

Wait! Wait! Wait! repeats the echo.

Polly knows that voice. She would recognize it anywhere! She has heard it in a tree's branches, floating through the sky, looking up at the stars. She has heard it laughing and crying and asking politely for more cake.

Polly turns her head and there is Buster. His paws are on his knees and he is trying desperately to catch his breath. Even though she is about to be munched up and swallowed by a revolting monster, a **bubble of laughter** and disbelief bursts up out of her chest. "Buster!" Polly yelps. "You're here! Oh, I *knew* you'd come!"

Buster holds up a paw to signal he needs a moment to get his breath back. "I. Really. Need. To. Exer … cise. More!" he pants.

The gorvan looks back at Polly, blinking its one red eye in a state of confusion. Finding not just one but *two* edible creatures in its lair was obviously not what it had been expecting when the stones called it back into the mines. Shrugging, it lifts Polly up to pop her into its dripping mouth.

"Wait!" yells Buster, standing up

straight. "Hey, you ugly big droop! Over here!"

The gorvan frowns and twists around to look at Buster, who is now jumping up and down and waving his hairy arms over his head.

"Gorvey! Hey!" he shouts. "Over here, you slimy snozzbooger! Look how big and fat and yummy I am! Don't eat that witch! Witches taste terrible! Believe me! I'm a monster. I should know." Then he does a pretend **wicked monstery laugh** to show that he really is a nasty witch-eating monster and not the completely crazy nutter that Polly knows he really is.

The gorvan blinks. Polly is not sure it understands what Buster is saying, but the whole weird situation is definitely confusing it. It frowns and another stream of purple slime drips down the front of its belly.

"Take me!" Buster shouts. "I'm yummy! Mmmmm …" he says, lifting up a hairy armpit and smelling underneath. "Delicious!"

"Buster!" Polly shouts. She can't believe what he's doing. He should be running away to safety, not hanging about to be gorvan food!

But the gorvan looks from one of them to another, blinking slowly. Its mouth drools more purple slime. Then it plops Polly on the ground and reaches for Buster. "Go!" yells Buster. And Polly instantly understands Buster's crazy plan. Clever, brave Buster.

253

Polly quickly stands up. She feels a familiar **hot rage** fill her body. Her fingertips **crackle** and **fizz** and she raises her arms up to strike the gorvan down, just as it wraps a tentacle around her best friend. "Leave. Him. Alone!" she roars without thinking. But as the heat of the spell fills her, Polly sees the gorvan expand. It gets bigger and darker and its eye flashes red and evil.

"Um … Polly?" Buster shouts. "I think you're making it bigger!"

The gorvan expands again and roars ferociously, its voice echoing loudly all throughout the chamber, and Polly realizes what she is doing. Of course! She should know this by now. Her anger is feeding the gorvan! It **roars** and **thrashes** its tentacles, swinging Buster around the chamber, smashing him against the stony walls.

"I'm OK!" Buster calls out. "I'm OK! But if you could do a spell soon, that would be great!"

Polly does her best to remain calm, but she can't bear watching the gorvan hurt her friend. Her heart jumps about like a rabbit. "Oh, Buster! I don't think I can do this!" she yells over the gorvan's roar. "I'm too scared!"

"About now would be good!" Buster yelps, just as the gorvan opens its enormous jaws once again. A wave of purple mist pours from its mouth.

Polly quickly closes her eyes and focuses on emptying all the fear and anger from her body. She knows there is no other way. She has to do the right spell – and now! She concentrates on slowing her heartbeat so that she can think clearly. Then she steps right up to the gorvan and stares into its boiling red eye.

I can do this! she tells herself. *I am a Silver Witch! Buster knows I can do this, Miss Spinnaker knows I can do this, Aunt Hilda knows I can do this. Even my father knew I could do this. This is what I have been called here to do. Me, Polly Proggett, Silver Witch. I can defeat this gorvan. I can! I can!*

Twenty-Three

Breathing deeply and blocking out the roaring of the gorvan and the yelps of her best friend, Polly draws a spell into her body. It rolls up into her chest like an ocean wave, cool and clean and blue, and fizzes in her fingertips. All around her, the chamber begins to rumble and shake. Pebbles and stones drop from the walls and roll about at her feet. The hairs on her arms stand up and her skin grows cool. She lifts her arms and a brilliant silver light flashes from her outstretched hands and surrounds the creature. She knows, even as it pours from her, that this is the biggest, most powerful spell she has ever done.

The gorvan blinks twice and drops Buster, who quickly scrambles out of the way. Polly holds the creature firm in her magic and sends the cool waves of her **kindness spell** into its boiling body over and over again. As she and Buster watch, the gorvan begins to **shrivel, hiss** and steam right before them. Bits of stone and metal lodged deep inside its slimy body drop away as it shrinks. Finally, just as Polly feels she can no longer hold on, it lets out a long, low sigh. Its tentacles shrink and its eye closes shut. Within moments all that is left of the terrifying creature is a small purple blob of slime glistening at Polly's feet.

"Whoa!" Buster says, staring at Polly and grinning widely. "You did it!" He pokes at the slime with a hairy toe. "You defeated a *gorvan*, Polly! That is SO cool! You are absolutely the most **amazing** witch that ever lived."

Polly crouches down to look at it more closely. Deep within its clear purple slime she can see the tiniest shadow of a heartbeat, pulsing rhythmically. Her own heart is still beating hard, but she feels calm and ever so slightly light-headed. "I don't think you can ever really kill them, Buster," she says, remembering what her father had told her, "just take away their power."

"My best friend defeated a gorvan!" Buster says, shaking his head and grinning proudly.

"I can't wait to tell everyone at school. They will definitely think witches are cool when I tell them about this!"

Polly gives Buster the **biggest hug ever.** "Anything for a friend," she giggles, pretending this is something she does every day. If she thinks about what she has done, it seems too unbelievable to be true. Is it really possible that she has defeated a *gorvan*? The most terrifying creature that ever lived? And just with kindness?

"We can tell them, right?" Buster says. "I mean, everyone knows gorvans exist now, don't they?"

"They sure do!" Polly smiles, remembering the chaos of the town square. "And, yes. No more secrets. Ever."

"Deal?" says Buster, happily, holding up a paw for a high five.

"Deal," says Polly, slapping his paw with her hand. "Anyway, how did you even get here?" she says, brushing dust off his fur. He has bruises all over his back, but otherwise he seems as happy as she's ever seen him. She feels it, too. The air is cleaner and clearer and easier to breathe, and all the purple mist has disappeared. "You can't have run all the way through the Amber Skull Forest?"

Buster grins. "Nope. A friend gave me a lift."

"A friend?" Polly says.

Buster nods. "Yes! You know them, too!"

Polly thinks for a while then shakes her head.

Nothing is coming to her. She can't think of a single monster who could get Buster to the mines so quickly.

Buster laughs. "I'll give you a clue: they can't *run*, but they can *fly*."

Polly screws up her face. "What are you talking about?" she says.

Buster rolls his eyes. "It's a *riddle*, Polly! They can't *run*, but they can *fly*," he says more slowly.

"I have no idea," Polly says, frowning.

Buster slaps his forehead. "From your *school*, Polly! She's waiting outside at the entrance to the mines with her mother's broomstick. Someone who can *fly*, but can't run. Because she broke her leg when the mines collapsed!"

Then Polly suddenly understands. "*Malorie*?" she says. "She *flew* you here?"

Buster nods. "She came to find me as soon as her mother got home and told her where you'd gone. She's pretty brave, you know. She's got a broken leg, but she can still fly a broomstick pretty well!"

Polly has a **funny feeling** in her belly. "But you don't even *like* broomstick rides!" she mumbles.

"Oh, Polly!" Buster laughs and Polly knows he understands what she is feeling. He always does. No matter how she might try and hide it. "You'll always be my *best* friend! But I can be friends with Malorie, too!"

"I'm not *jealous* if that's what you're thinking!" Polly grumbles, looking around for a flat stone, even though what she is saying is not exactly true. Buster has always been *her* special friend. She can't imagine what it would feel like to share him with someone else. But then she realizes that the more witches who are friends with monsters, the better it will be for everyone. And she decides that maybe Buster and Malorie being friends could be a good thing, after all. Maybe this is even the sign of a new future for Blackmoon Coven?

Eventually, Polly finds what she's looking for and scoops up the sticky purple blob onto a thin piece of slate. It wobbles like jelly and lets off a hiss of steam.

Buster giggles quietly and follows her into the dark red cave. "Whoa," he says, looking at the sparkly things more closely.

"Don't touch anything," Polly warns him. She drops the blob of slime onto a shelf. It slithers toward the back of the ledge and flattens itself against the rippling red wall. "Surely *now* Blackmoon Coven will go back to how it was before?" she wonders aloud, looking around at the pulsating red cave.

"I hope so!" Buster says.

"Hey, maybe you'll be able to get your medal ceremony after all!" says Polly.

"Oh yeah!" says Buster happily. "And the special afternoon tea!"

"And the special afternoon tea," she says, smiling.

"Can we maybe invite Malorie?" Buster asks, shyly.

"Of course," Polly assures him. "And her family, too."

"Not Mrs. Halloway?" Buster gasps, his eyes wide. "She *hates* monsters. She thinks they're dangerous and noisy and smelly!"

"Well, you are the perfect monster to prove her wrong then, aren't you?" Polly says. "Especially if you are friends with her daughter!"

"Ha!" Buster chuckles. "I guess so!" But when he thinks Polly isn't looking, he takes a quick sniff under one armpit just to check.

"Come on," Polly says, taking Buster's paw and pretending not to notice. "Let's go. This is a horrible place." She shivers as they step out of the cave. "Let's hope we never have to ever come here again."

"Never *ever!*" agrees Buster.

Polly takes a deep breath and recites the *gorvan's spell* for the last time. Slowly, noisily, the wall rumbles back into place, sealing the cave behind it. She and Buster stand side by side in the echoey dark. Soon, all she can hear is Buster's quiet breathing and all she can feel is his big warm paw in her small cool hand. And she knows they are alone.

Polly knows her dad can't see her anymore,

but she hopes that somehow, somewhere, wherever he might be, he can sense that it is all over. And that he is feeling proud.

She thinks of him and smiles.

Twenty-Four

Polly and Buster sit together on the podium, looking out over the crowd. All of Blackmoon Coven is gathered in the town square for the Mayor's medal ceremony and the sun is shining brightly for the first time in days.

Usually only a handful of witches turn up to these events, but this is the first time a monster is going to receive an award and so the monsters' side of the square is packed. Some of the witches and warlocks glance at them suspiciously, but the monsters stand tall and fiercely proud that one of their own is finally getting recognized.

Polly and Buster's faces have been splashed all over the newspapers and television screens that week, as the "runaway heroes who saved Blackmoon Coven," and even Malorie got a mention for transporting Buster to the action just in time. More importantly, articles about the bravery of the witches and monsters defeating the gorvan by working together have been published all around the country.

Even the Amber Skull Forest Gang appeared

in a glowing article for their part in defending the town from the beastly menace, which up until then no one had quite believed really existed. Every single witch, warlock and monster in the square today knows how lucky they are to be there when they had come so close to losing everything to the gorvan.

Buster's mother and father are seated in the front row, of course, in the chairs lined up for special friends and family. His mother is dressed in her finest teapot hat and is almost bursting out of her fancy red-and-yellow floral dress with **pride**. She keeps turning around and whispering to anyone who will listen, "That's my son up there. That's my son!"

His father, squeezed into his only suit of brown polyester and shiny black shoes, sits there frowning importantly as the doodle band **honks** and **bleats** in the background.

On the other side of the aisle sit Polly's sister and mother. As the Mayor's special guests, they are also dressed in their very best witch clothes of black and gray, **ceremonial pointy hats** on their laps, even though they are unsure of Polly's role in today's proceedings. Everyone knows the Mayor only gives out one medal every few months, and everyone knows this medal is going to Buster. Despite everything that's happened, there are still some witches who don't think a monster should receive a medal. But everyone has been warned that there will be a special announcement as well as the medal ceremony this afternoon, and somehow Polly has something to do with it. So the whole town has turned up to find out the surprise.

Polly knows that her special invitation to the Mayor's proceedings is the only reason her mother has held off grounding her for life, and for this she will always be grateful. Whether she will be accepted back into Miss Madden's is something her headmistress is still yet to decide, but at this stage, Polly doesn't care. Buster is getting a hero's honor, and that's all that matters to her anyway.

Besides, she's not sure she wants to go to Miss Madden's anymore – not now that Miss Spinnaker no longer teaches there. Miss Spinnaker has already mentioned she is thinking of starting her *own* school of magic, out of town, with an old friend of hers.

Polly sees her favorite teacher standing on tippy-toes in the crowd, and her heart flutters with joy to see who is beside her. Aunt Hilda has come all this way especially, just to see Buster receive his medal, and has promised Polly she will stay for the celebratory afternoon tea. Miss Spinnaker gives Aunt Hilda a smile, and Polly's aunt returns it. Polly has only just discovered that Aunt Hilda and Miss Spinnaker were best friends at school. Her cheeks **warm with happiness** as she sees Miss Spinnaker hug Aunt Hilda. They both look up toward the stage as the Mayor clears her throat into the microphone.

Mayor Redwolf's cape billows around her silver-buckled boots, and Polly sees she has a *red velvet medal box* in her bejeweled right hand. Polly's heart starts to beat faster and she reaches for Buster's paw. She can feel his palm is hot and sweaty, too, and he grins at her nervously. The band stops playing and an expectant hush falls over the crowd. But before the Mayor speaks, she beckons for someone else to come and stand beside her.

A wave of surprised murmuring rolls across the crowd when they see who it is. Carmen, the leader of the Amber Skull Forest Gang, walks up to stand beside Mayor Redwolf on the stage. Polly sucks in a breath of surprise to see how powerful and strong the two leaders look standing there, side by side, and she gazes at them both in admiration. Like everyone else gathered in the square today, she has no idea why Carmen is up there.

The rumble of voices grows louder and louder as the witches and monsters in the crowd try to work out what is going on. Mayor Redwolf lifts up one hand to quiet them.

"As you know," she begins, in her deep,

loud voice, "we are gathered here to award Blackmoon Coven's most prestigious medal for bravery to our very first monster recipient, Buster Grewclaw."

An **almighty cheer** goes up from the monster side of the crowd and someone lets off a very noisy peeplepopper that spins and fizzes above their heads. It bounces off the horns of a tall monster, who gives an indignant shout.

The Mayor lifts her hand again. "But many of you will also know our dear Buster is only one part of an extraordinarily brave duo, who worked fearlessly together to defeat the gorvan, once and for all. Can we also give a big round of applause to our other young hero …

Polly Proggett!"

Polly feels herself blushing as the witch side of the crowd roars even louder than the monsters. Her mother wipes a tear from her eye and Polly watches Winifred gesture to her school friends that Polly is *her* sister.

But there is only one medal in her hand, Polly thinks. *Why is the Mayor even mentioning me?*

"However, what I wish to celebrate today," the Mayor continues, "even more than the bravery these young heroes displayed, is their deep and long-standing friendship. I believe these two friends, Polly and Buster, have served to remind us of what Blackmoon Coven was always meant to be: a home for both witches *and* monsters to enjoy, living together peacefully. As *equals*."

There is an uncomfortable shuffling in the crowd. A few monsters and witches glance sideways at each other, unsure of the direction this ceremony is taking. They want to know now – and the wait is making them slightly irritable – is it *Buster* who is going to receive the medal, or has the Mayor decided to give it to Polly? Is today a day for *monsters* to celebrate? Or witches?

"As Mayor of Blackmoon Coven," she says, "it is my job to make the laws and decisions that I believe best serve the interests of our inhabitants. But it has been brought to my attention that there is no way, as a witch, I can represent the needs of *all* of our community, in particular those of our monster friends. Therefore, I have invited Carmen Magniflora, leader of the Amber Skull Forest Gang, to rule Blackmoon Coven alongside me."

For a startled moment, the square is so quiet, Polly can hear Buster's tummy rumbling, and she squeezes his paw a little tighter. She watches the look of shock flower across all the upturned faces in the crowd as, one by one, they understand what Mayor Redwolf is saying.

Blackmoon Coven ruled by a *monster*? But that's *never* happened in its entire history! Even the monsters in the crowd look bamboozled.

But then,
from right in the middle of
all the shock-stilled bodies,
Polly hears a slow
clap begin.

And when she spots where the noise is coming from she sees it is Milly, her big ginger-speckled head poking up above the crowd. She wipes a tear from her eye and nods appreciatively at Polly and Buster. *You did it!* Polly sees Milly whisper. *You started a revolution!*

Polly's eyes **prickle with tears.** Soon, more and more monsters join in Milly's slow clap and then witches and warlocks, too, until the entire crowd is clapping and nodding and wiping away tears as they understand what this means for the monsters living in Blackmoon Coven. Finally, they will have someone leading their town who understands what life is like for *them*.

Mayor Redwolf takes Carmen's paw in her hand and holds it up high. Then Polly sees something she never dreamed would happen …

Her mom places her hat on the ground, and crosses the aisle to stand in front of Buster's mother. Mrs. Grewclaw looks confused, but then Polly's mother mumbles something, smiles warmly and holds out a hand. Mrs. Grewclaw's eyes grow wide. She wipes both her paws against her skirt, and stands up to take Polly's mother's outstretched hand. Together they face the crowd, holding their hands up in the air for all to see, then turn and hug each other.

Witches, warlocks and monsters cheer wildly and a **laughing sob** bursts from Polly's chest.

As she watches from the stage, one by one, witches and monsters cross the square to hug each other, many of them sobbing or laughing uproariously. Polly even spots Mrs. Halloway being lovingly squeezed by a big furry monster. Malorie stands beside them, laughing, before she is pulled into the hug, too. It is the best thing Polly has ever seen.

She knows now, for sure, the gorvan's evil mist has well and truly gone from Blackmoon Coven.

Twenty-Five

*F*inally, when all has settled down and everyone is seated again, Mayor Redwolf beckons for Polly and Buster to join her and Carmen at the front of the stage. Mayor Redwolf opens the red velvet box she's been holding, then lifts out a large gold disk on a long gold chain from where it is nestled in its purple satin bed.

The Mayor holds the chain up over Buster's head and places it around his broad neck. His cheeks **bloom pink** and he **swells with happiness,** the buttons on his suit jacket popping off all over the stage. The townsfolk **laugh** and **cheer** and **whistle.** Buster waves and the crowd chants his name. "Buster! Buster! Buster!" – the first monster ever in the history of Blackmoon Coven to receive a medal. He has become so **swollen with pride** that Polly has to grab his paw to stop him floating off the stage. He gives Polly a massive hug, which makes her giggle, and the crowd roars again.

"Congratulations, Buster Grewclaw," shouts Mayor Redwolf into the microphone, shushing the crowd so they'll pay attention to what she has to say next. "Our town is a happier, safer place thanks to you, and this medal is mightily deserved. But we have one more member of our town to reward today and for you, Polly, we have had another token of our appreciation made especially. I would like to ask my colleague, as our monster representative of this town, if she would mind doing the honors in her new role as … Mayor Magniflora."

Carmen smiles and steps up to the microphone, her emerald-green eyes sliding toward Polly as she speaks. "Thank you, Mayor

Redwolf. It is an honor to serve this town alongside you and an even greater honor to present this award in my first act as Mayor." She takes out another red velvet box from her pocket and pulls out a *gold disk* on a long gold chain, very similar to Buster's, then beckons for Polly to step closer. "Can you please put your hands together for the bravest nine-year-old witch in all of Blackmoon Coven!" she shouts above all the wild cheering. "Polly Proggett, vanquisher of gorvans and friend of monsters!"

Polly's head **spins dizzily** as the crowd roars. She hears voices she recognizes and Buster's happy rumbling beside her. Carmen bends down to look deep into Polly's eyes.

"This unity in our town is all thanks to you, Polly," she says in her low, growly voice, close to Polly's ear so that she can be heard above all the noise. "This medal is only a small symbol of everything you have helped us believe in through your courage and kindness." She holds it up so that Polly can examine the medal more closely. "Look," she says. "I have had it made especially for you, Polly."

She points at the middle of Polly's medal with one long claw and taps at a bright-red stone embedded there.

Polly looks at Carmen, her eyes wide and her stomach curling. "That's ... that's not a gorvan's stone, is it?" she gasps, quickly stepping back.

Carmen shakes her head and chuckles. "Oh no, Polly. I think we have all learned our lesson there! This is a *goblin's gem*. They are as rare as gorvan's stones and as difficult to find. This gem has been passed down through generations of monsters in my family and, once activated, carries magic even greater than that of a gorvan's stone. We have been searching for the right witch to give it to for a long time. I had thought, at first, it might have been Miss Spinnaker, but she assured me that it wasn't her. She told me, only days after your spell in the gallery, dear Polly, that she believed the witch we were waiting for was on her way. And here you are."

Polly looks up at Carmen, her eyes wide. Carmen smiles, her sharp teeth glinting in the sunlight. "Don't worry. It hasn't yet been activated. Touch it. You will see it is cool, not warm. But one day, dear Polly, as the town's first true Silver Witch, we may need you to once again lead us out of trouble. And you may need this gem. So Mayor Redwolf and I have decided this is meant for you. You have proven yourself worthy."

Carmen slips the chain over Polly's head to the noise of cheering in the background. Polly looks out at the crowd. She knows they think she has only received a medal of honor. Not a magic gem with power even greater than the gorvan's stones! She seeks out Miss Spinnaker's face and sees her teacher smile knowingly and proudly.

Polly looks down at the medal. The ruby-red gem *glints* from the golden disk, and she suddenly feels so much older than her nine short years. *I don't know if I want this!* she thinks. But she knows she doesn't have a choice. As her aunt had told her: sometimes you don't get to choose who you are in life. Life just chooses you.

"Guard this with your life, Polly," Carmen murmurs into her ear, "and if ever the need should arise, use it wisely. We trust you, brave Silver Witch. Don't let us down."

Then Carmen walks over to stand beside Mayor Redwolf. Buster takes Polly's hand. All around the square, Polly sees witches standing beside monsters, looking up at her with faces full of hope. And she realizes that this is what she has created. She, Polly Proggett, has done something more powerful than any witch's magic. She has created this **feeling of good.**

Polly closes her other hand over the disk hanging around her neck. She understands now that there will always be bad things below them, deep in the earth. Sleeping, rumbling, able to be woken at any time. She knows now that both things are powerful: love and hate. Both can rule the world.

But when her time comes, she knows which
she will choose.

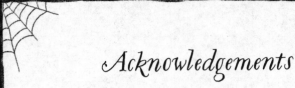

Acknowledgements

I write for children because they are the best people in the world. They care about kindness, fairness and all the things that really matter, and when they love something, they love it with every bit of their hearts. I have received so much love for Polly and Buster; letters, drawings and photographs, and every single one fills me with joy and gratitude. And on writing days when the story doesn't work, or the words get stuck, or everything just feels too hard, I think of all of you waiting impatiently to find out what Polly and Buster get up to next, and I make myself sit back down again until the story comes. So, thank you. You make me want to be the best writer I can be.

I feel so lucky to have so many wonderful kids in my life, but there are a few I want to mention by name: Will and Amber for the Polly and Buster song, Arabella for her wonderful feedback, and Cliona for taking my books all the way to Ireland with her. But my biggest thanks go to all the Bennie St. kids for making me feel so welcome: Polly, Abbey and Baby Taraji (even though she still prefers to chew my books) and especially Greer, Abel and Bede for the cards, cuddles and monster jamcakes. You have made me feel like this is where I belong.

About Sally Rippin

Sally Rippin is the sort of grown-up who remembers exactly what it was like to be a kid. That's one of the reasons her books are so beloved around the world. She has written more than sixty books for children, including the best-selling *Billie B. Brown* and *Hey Jack!* series. Sally's books have sold over four million copies internationally, which is enough to make any monster puff up with happiness.

HAVE YOU READ THE ENTIRE POLLY AND BUSTER SERIES?

BOOK ONE

☐

BOOK TWO

☐

BOOK THREE

☑